Days in the Life

A collection of short stories

TONY LINDSELL

Days in the Life

DEDICATION

For my parents, James and Curlie, and for Victoria,
Jonathan and Heleni

Days in the Life

CONTENTS

Days in the Life

ACKNOWLEDGMENTS

With thanks to Steve Calcutt and all the members, past and present, of the Anubis creative writing group, Leamington Spa, and to Connie Bott and her creative writing group in Warwick, all of whose constant encouragement, constructive feedback and good cheer has motivated and inspired me.

Days in the Life

Days in the Life

1. TEOFILA AND I

Francoise dumped me, feet first, in the snow. Disrespectful cow. It was not as if she didn't know my history – some of it anyway. She'd heard it often enough.

Then, of all things, she stood on me, her boot-clad feet drenching me, and fiddled around with a metal box on top of the bus stop. She appeared to be checking some dials. A man was looking on, waiting, his skis upright against his shoulder. His head was tilted to one side, as if studying something. He looked slightly bemused.

"L'autobus…" she said to him with a shrug, as if that would explain everything.

I was shivering, I can tell you, quite out of my comfort zone, all these cars streaming past throwing slush all over me. Eventually the bus came. She got on, carrying me, and he got on too. The cheek of the woman – she just plonked me down in the dripping aisle, abandoned me there and started chatting to the driver, a stinking Gauloise in her mouth as if it wouldn't kill her. Probably thought it made her look elegant.

The man was staring at me and when the bus reached Jaillet and she moved to get off, clasping my back, he followed.

"I'd like to buy your chair," he said as he stepped onto the pavement, pointing to me.

"Excusez-moi?"

She put me down with a bit of a jolt.

"It know it is a very unusual request but I would like to buy your chair."

I was horrified. It was not that I held any loyalty to Francoise or even, any longer, to Isabelle. Indeed life had become quite boring and predictable recently and I was keen for a new adventure, but the thought of going off with this stranger... I mean, he didn't even sound French. I suppose it was not impossible that he would take me home to Italy, but what if he took me to some foreign country?

Fortunately I was relieved of my immediate worries.

"It is not mine," she said. "It is my sister Isabelle's. You will have to ask her and she can tell you about it."

Ah well, at least she did remember that I was not just some common or garden piece of mass-produced riff-raff.

"You can come with me, if you wish," she said. "We live just down this street."

She half-dragged me over the ice and slush on the pavement, scratching my shins. Really, she was the end. I suppose I must not be too hard on her what with the illness setting in. But she can be quite maddening sometimes, so inconsiderate. Surely the bus company could provide her with some steps or something – I certainly would not wish to come out here in the snow again.

But the man - I was beginning to warm to him.

"Let me carry the chair for you," he said, as charming

as you like. And she, not giving a jot that he was already carrying his skis, handed me over to him with barely a *merci*.

This was much more comfortable, though I was a little afraid that if the man slipped on some ice, we'd all go crashing down - him, the skis, the sticks and me.

Isabelle appeared as we reached the door.

"What are you doing with my chair?" she exclaimed, horrified, when she saw the state of me. "Francoise, that is my Italian chair."

"He wants to buy it," said Francoise. She clumped a trail of snow across the carpet, pulling the beret from her head to reveal the short hair growing back.

Isabelle looked at her, then puffed her lips and shoulders in resignation as only the French can. She is a woman of some years now, nine years older than me of course, yet still elegant and slim.

"Je m'appelle Isabelle," she said, turning to the man. "My name is Isabelle."

She did not seem surprised to see him. I suppose, living with Francoise, nothing would surprise you.

"Please – sit." She gestured towards me. "Café?"

"Thank you. Merci. Very comfortable," he said.

"Indeed."

The man had a gentle touch and I folded around him. I could sense him looking about the room. Isabelle's taste was eclectic, to put it politely, but I was so used to living there that I barely noticed it now.

In the corner sat a large fat Buddha, polished to such a shine that you could admire yourself in the folds of its golden stomach. On one wall hung a painting of the Italian house and on another the head of a fierce-looking wildebeest, its horns forming a halo, only half-expressed. A soft doll troubadour, an orange cape over checked green trousers, strummed a mandolin in the corner of a chaise longue. The chaise longue was embroidered in silver, the upholstery a darker shade of burgundy. We looked down, of course, on these upholstered cousins, not that they knew it. They thought that they were the height of fashion and refinement. They pictured themselves as those who reclined on them – 1930's starlets in diaphanous silk dresses, cigarette holder in hand and smoke swirling in the sunlight.

But these cousins would be talking thin air and chitter-chat. They would not know the hours of concentration and toil, of grief and love, of study, thought and inspiration, the sweet moments of peace, that one of us could bring.

"I am sorry," he said. "My French is not good. Parlez-vous anglais?"

He stretched out the 's', but I forgave him.

"A little," she said. "I will try. So, dites-moi - tell me - why do you want to buy this chair? It is a strange request, no?"

The man seemed to go into a dream and did not speak. It was an awkward moment. I stared at the painting of the house in Tuscany. Teofila, my twin sister, and I were in it, bathed in sunlight. We were on the terrazza, looking east across the little wood and the mountains. I remembered the morning when I first woke there, the glorious smell of new wood merging into the tang of the hill country and the games Isabelle used to play with her brother Marco. Poor Marco – he didn't stand a chance when they bombed Milano in '43. Francoise was not even born yet.

I could recall as if it was yesterday the laughs we had, Teofila and I, about the fancy chairs in the other rooms and their airs and graces - I would giggle and giggle when she imitated their stuffy accents and their routine ways;

they would look so miffed, whenever we found ourselves in the same room, as we chuckled and joked and stole their limelight.

And then - much later, after Isabelle had come back to find me in '45 - the frightful journey here, alone now: the time they took to pack me up; the awful stuffy box - I nearly suffocated in that straw with all the irritating little insects that lived in it; the bumpy ride across the hill to the road on the back of a cart, two old black cobs snorting and stamping, protesting and lurching at every step -it was most uncomfortable; and the long slow haul in the back of a stinking Fiat truck through Tuscany, across Piedmont and finally into France. At times I thought I would die of ennui, as they say in this country, or else suffocate from the exhaust fumes.

But above everything, the memories came flooding back of the war years, and of Charles and Effie.

My darling wife, there is not a moment of every day when I am not thinking of you. Even when the C.O. is talking to me, I feel you with me. When I remember the party the evening before we were married, I pinch myself. You looked so beautiful coming down the stairs in your white gown, your auburn hair gathered in a coronet. For several moments I could not breathe and could not understand how a man could be so lucky.

Poor George got it in the neck today. They say he'll be fine though he might lose the use of his right arm. Silly bugger. Still, I told him to invite you to a good restaurant when he's fixed up and back in town. I don't know whether we'll see him again out here – though he barely got here.

I remember that letter so clearly. Charles, or to give him his full name, Major Charles Stone, was sitting on me, his back hunched over his notepad. He was a tall man, good-looking, everyone said, with that Roman nose and angular jaw, dark hair swept back and already greying.

Reserved, I would say. Not a man who would normally allow his feelings to get the better of him. But on this day, I could feel a few tears fall on me and saw many more fall on his letter. I knew, from his conversations, that George was a friend from childhood. They'd joined the regiment together and I suppose that war, in all its parts, had thrown him.

"It reminds me of something," said the man eventually, seeming to wake.

"It is a very special chair to our family, to me especially," said Isabelle.

"Why is that?"

"This chair was – how you say in English? – was fabriquee, was carved, by my grandfather Leonardo. He was Italian, a man who loved wood. Books and wood. 'Isabelle,' he would say, 'This wood does not grow old like me. This wood will be with you and your children.'

"He had built a workshop in a stone barn on his land in the mountains north of Florence where pigs once lived. He took the bare trunks from trees that fell, beech and scented cypress, and hewed them into planks and then into shapes like a sculptor from marble. Sometimes he would just carve a figure - a dancer, a discus thrower or a lover. And other times he would make something practical – a card table, a fruit bowl or a chair. Nothing was the same.

"He was a quiet man, he did not shout. He had the air of someone who knew where he was going, even in his eighties. He had wild grey hair that did not often see a barber and skin burnt to the terracotta of the land there. He would wear a pair of blue dungarees whatever the weather and whatever the company. In summer, there would be nothing between the top of the dungarees and his skin, and in winter there would be a thick red shirt, or maybe two when the snow was on the ground and progress to the barn was treacherous and slow.

"His Dalmatian bitch Gabbia never left his side, shuffling and pushing to be in the limelight. But when it came to the machines, she somehow knew to stand back. Grandfather always had a cigarette hanging from his lips. A Camel. He would get them in from Rome. Somehow it would stay there, even if he spoke. All his works, everything he made, had that lingering smell of Camel about them. Even this chair that you wish to buy. For him the smell of the Camel tobacco was art, was part and parcel of the creation. "

The man stood up. He lifted me and sniffed. It was most unseemly, but he appeared pleased, wafting me across his nose like the bouquet of some fine wine.

"A hint," he said politely

My darling Charles

Aren't we so lucky to have such a love? I have received your letters no.'s 41 and 42 and feel so happy that finally you and all the 1ˢᵗ Herts are able to show them what you are made of. And at the same time, my darling, I am so worried for you. Do please look after yourself, dearest. The tide is turning and Mr Hitler is running in several directions. It will surely not be too long now before we are back together. Wouldn't it be so wonderful to have children? I envisage, my darling Charles, such a wonderful life for us when this awful war is over.

Charles had read and re-read this one. I could almost picture Effie back there in England in her ATS uniform - beautiful, innocent and fearful. The previous week, I had heard one of the men working on the electricity outside ask the Sergeant, 'What is Effie short for, anyway, Sarge?'

'Effin' gorgeous, I imagine, mate,' came the reply, accompanied by a hearty guffaw.

Isabelle brushed a stray hair from her forehead.

"One day," she said, "Grandfather called to me. 'Isa,

let us go to the barn and make some chairs for you. We will make two chairs – twins. They will be made from the finest wood. Their back legs will have the strength of an ox and will stand the sternest test; and their front legs will have the grace of a ballet dancer. Their seats will be of firm, soft wicker. On the front legs and on the back I will carve a design. What design will you choose?' I don't know why, but I chose a dragon for the legs, and an apple for the back."

The man leant down, studying me again. He looked at the dragon's head that sits in the centre of each of my front legs, its tongue of fire curling around the upper part; and at the apples that sit on either side of my back.

"There, you see?"

"Indeed", he said. "Unique."

"Yes," she said. "Unique. The twin chair had lemons instead of apples."

Ah yes, my dear sister, Teofila. I was the better-looking, though I say so myself. She tended to fret and worry as she got older, and over the years her wood faded and split while mine shone. She told me not to read Charles' letters, but I couldn't help it. I just like to understand my guests.

My darling Effie

I feel so proud. The C.O. has given me command of 2 Company and our orders were to take a hill from the Boche. We came at them from a direction they did not expect. They ran like jack rabbits. I feel that I avenged for George and maybe many others . At last I felt that I was doing something useful in this war.

(I can tell you, Charles was puffed up like a peacock when he came back from that little operation and briefed the C.O.)

We went into Florence for dinner last week. It was wonderful to sit at a table with a red-checked table cloth, to drink wine and be served and to have a proper shave and a bath in the city. How awful the mud is on the front line – it is grey, almost blue, and sticks to everything when it is wet.

"The two chairs lived in the hallway of my grandfather's house," Isabelle went on, "Or sometimes out on the terrazza. Whenever I visited, I would sit in them. When the war came, the house was occupied first by the Germans and then later by the British as they advanced north against the Gothic Line. With all the fighting, Grandfather had to move down to Fiesole and leave the house - and of course the chairs - behind."

We were taken to the library when the Brits took over the villa. The C.O. insisted that only upright chairs be in the room. He called it his command room. 'No slouching,' he would say. 'Always alert'. It was a grand room. Arched mahogany bookshelves lined three walls and the panels above them, before the wood-lined ceiling, depicted scenes of a dancer. She wore a sequinned, mauve tulle that whirled and swirled with every panel of her whirling and swirling until her breathless bow in the far corner of the room.

One of my cousins had taken up position close to one end. He, for I assumed that he was a he, was the biggest cousin I had ever met - a sofa wide enough for five people to sit across should they so have wished. He was upholstered in leather, now tanned and cracked. A burgundy rug lay over his surface, and on it a single book. I expected the book to be some learned tome but when I looked more closely, I saw that it was entitled 'English Country Gardens'.

The fourth wall was not really a wall. It was for the most part a huge window, from ceiling to floor. A curtain that must have been twenty feet high hung from an ornate metal rail. The window looked out north towards the mountains.

Days in the Life

My sister and I were there in the library as usual on 18 October 1944. Charles walked in and drew me up to the table as was his wont. He had received an envelope and I could see from the handwriting that it was from Effie.

My dearest Charles

I have some wonderful news, my darling, or I pray that I do. I think we are going to have a baby! You see, I have missed my last two monthlies, my darling. I did not want to raise your hopes until I was nearly sure, but now I am and I believe that wonderful night in the Swan Hotel was even more wonderful than we first imagined. Can you believe it, my love? I wonder will it be a boy or a girl. I long for you to come home so that you can be with me and the baby as it grows. I know that you must do all that is required of you, my love, but please please do not do anything rash. According to Mr Churchill, this war will soon be won. We will have to think about a house now darling – for three!

He'd barely taken it in when the C.O. entered.

'We have a problem, Charles. Lieutenant Jackson took Point 677 this morning, but an enemy patrol counter-attacked. He's wounded and we've lost other men. I need you to lead a relief party. Get armed men and ammunition and a rations party up to them immediately.'

'Yes sir,' said Charles. 'I…I have some good news.'

'Tell me later,' said the C.O. brusquely, waving his arm aside. 'No delay.'

******

The day wore on and no word came through. The C.O. had been pacing up and down the command room for some hours. Sometimes he would stop and stare out of the vast window, searching, it seemed, for any kind of message. It was late in the evening when Charles came back. Captain Evans was with him. They were ashen-faced, drained, their uniforms torn and smeared with blood and soil. Charles seemed barely able to raise his arm in a salute.

'Sit down, Charles,' the C.O. said gently, waving his arm towards me. 'A quick debrief and then the medics will sort you out.'

As he sat, I could feel blood oozing from his thigh, warm and thick. His voice was halting and he seemed to be grabbing for breath.

'The artillery were firing as planned, sir, but the shells were not clearing the mountain, they were falling amongst us. Everyone scattered. We lost Sergeant Whiting and other men. We could not get through to the artillery on the wireless to tell them to stop. We pressed forward again and the same thing happened. By the time we got close to Point 677, we realised the Boche had re-occupied it. They opened fire - I took a hit in my thigh. I sent Captain Evans forward with the spare ammunition and remaining armed men to try to reach Jackson.' Charles faltered like a dying battery. He wiped his palm across his forehead. 'They were met with a hail of grenades…he was the only man who made it. He had no option but to retreat. I managed to bring those of the ration party that were left back, sir, but twenty-three men are missing and there are five stretcher cases.'

'Dear God,' said the C.O.

'I'm sorry, sir.' It was barely a whisper.

I could feel Charles' energy leaving him as he slumped against me, fainting. I was relieved to see the Medical Officer arrive and examine him there and then.

'It is not one wound. There are seven.' He shouted for an orderly. 'We need to get his thigh stitched; he's losing too much blood.'

Most of that blood was on me. It seeped into my being and to this day you can see it, a darker shadow down my right side.

The orderlies lifted Charles onto a stretcher, for some reason picking up my sister, turning her on her back for support beneath the canvas, and heading off for the Field Hospital the other side of the small wood that bordered the property. I thought that that was the end of it, that at least now Charles was safe in medical care.

Boom! An air-splitting explosion outside shattered the silence that was left in the room. Splinters and shrapnel peppered the side of the house. A rushing crescendo of sound followed, as if a great wave were breaking on a dry beach.

'What in heaven's name?' said the C.O.

Captain Evans came back in. He looked devastated, lost.

'A shell sir, a stray shell out of nowhere, exploded in the tree. Blew the top of the tree apart. Half the trunk and all the branches landed on Major Stone and the orderlies. The blast and the tree, sir, they had no chance.'

The C.O. sat down on me, his head in his hands, oblivious to the sticky blood seeping into his trousers, all that was left now of Charles.

I felt sick. So much death, so close. Charles had become, for me, a friend but my grief for him was outweighed by my grief not just for Teofila but for Effie. I wanted to reach out to her, to console her, to tell her how brave her Charles had been, how happy he had been when he received the letter. But now, I thought, she will just receive a sterile, stereotyped letter from the British King saying how grateful he had been for Charles' selfless service - and she would bring up a child alone.

"When the war ended," said Isabelle, "I went to Italy

with my mother. Grandfather had become very frail and had not returned from Fiesole. We went up to the house. My heart lurched when I saw the shutters swinging open, weeds growing on the terrazza and the roof collapsed on Grandfather's stone barn. A large section of the wood was razed to the ground, the jagged stump of one tree standing defiantly against the destruction. I feared that everything in the house would be ransacked or ruined. I went straight to the library. The books were still on their shelves and though a thick film of dust lay over the floor and the kitchen table, which for some reason had been moved in there, the room was undamaged. Except for one thing - only one of the chairs was there. A dark stain marked its right side, but otherwise it was fine. I searched high and low for the other chair, the one with the lemons, but there was no sign of it.

So, you understand, this chair is very special to me."

The man nodded. He reached his left hand across to the inside pocket of his ski jacket and pulled out a wallet. He extracted a dog-eared black and white photograph and handed it to Isabelle.

Two men in battle dress were seated on the terrace of a house looking out over hills.

"Mon Dieu! That is my grandfather's house. These are the chairs," she gasped.

I recognised myself and my sister immediately – the dragons on our legs stood out clearly. The men – Charles and George, of course – were smoking. Charles seemed to be leaning forward to make a point and I could just make out the apple on my back.

"My name is Simon Stone," said the man. "This one," he paused, pointing to Charles, "is my father."

Days in the Life

2 HARLEQUINS

They came in two by two. He didn't notice the first ones. Only the bodies – the dead ones on the basin.

He swept them away to the floor, barely thinking. He looked up. In the corner of the aperture, where the sloping section of roof in the old house met the window frame, two of them appeared from a tiny crevice. The hole, he thought, was too small to accommodate their bodies, but that, clearly, was not what they thought.

Like bubbles of stinking methane, the memories he'd tried to shut away for so long, things he could never speak about to anyone, swarmed from the swamp of his life.

A ladybird landed, wings wide and innocent, on his hand as he lay in the long grass. Those days were untroubled – the sky blue, the weather warm, the grass swaying in a breeze that he did not feel. Untroubled, that is, except for his sister, Desdemona. Dezzy, her friends called her, but he called her Demona. Demona who was so fucking dumb, and so fucking gorgeous.

She was there in the garden too. She was there singing, in her lilting pixie-like song, 'Ladybird, ladybird, fly away home, your house is on fire and your children will burn.'

There was another verse that she made up. 'Ladybird, ladybird take to the sky, fly up to the clouds, fly ever so high.'

He changed the second line.

'Ladybird, ladybird take to the sky, fly back to your house and watch your children fry.'

"That's mean," Demona said.

It was meant to be.

That was the children stuff.

These ladybirds were different. They had more spots and were bigger. Their red had an orange about it and they carried a sinister black hood. He remembered reading about them in some cast-away red top in the dentist's waiting-room. 'STD-riddled ladybirds invade UK,' screamed the headline. 'Asian insects spreading faster than grey squirrels.' Harlequin ladybirds they were called.

He hunted around the bookshelves until he found it - A Field Guide to the Insects of Great Britain. The sexual appetite of harlequins was voracious, the book said, and could be satisfied by any passing fellow insect. They did indeed carry STD's, but transmitted them only between themselves. Infected insects carried tiny yellow fungi on their wings.

Acne. Livid, cream-yellow pustules disrupting her perfect features.

'Septic', he would call her. 'Leper'… 'carbuncle'…'scabious'. He would vie with himself to find the word that would hurt her the most.

That was still the teenage stuff, the sibling stuff.

When he returned to the bathroom, there were more of them. They marched down the wall, still two by two, in a curving column. A few had reached the soap. He studied them closely. Sure enough, some of them carried a pin of yellow on their wings. There is nothing to worry about if a lot of them want to take up residence in the warmth of your bedroom, said the guide.

In my bedroom? You're having a laugh.

"Sorry, mate," he said, as he rinsed the soap under the hot tap. He watched as the insects struggled briefly to gain a foothold on the basin before plunging, like climbers on a sheer rockface, down the plug hole.

Now, he opened the window. He took an old magazine, the Sunday Times colour supplement - a picture of Posh Spice on the front - and swept it up the wall. Some of the ladybirds crowded onto it, others fell into the basin. He flicked the magazine out of the window and a red swirl fell, then rose, in the autumn air.

He found, when he looked back, that the magazine had squashed some of them. Tiny traces of yellow blood smeared the wall and Posh's face, and the occasional wing, torn from its owner, clung limply to the plaster.

An arrangement in the blood, the thumbnail foetus distinct and accusing. He got away with it. No one questioned his role in it, but she was a broken woman afterwards. Never married, never had another child. She moved away and lived for years in seclusion. He made a show of being the heartbroken elder brother when she died.

That was the adult stuff.

He took a rag and cleaned off the paint. He threw Posh in the recycling bin. Something itched at the back of his neck, above his collar. He cuffed his hand across. A harlequin landed on the floorboards.

'Fuck you,' it seemed to say, prancing around, oblivious of his swipe. 'You can't get rid of me that easily.' He glared at it, wondering what orgies it had enjoyed the night before. That morning perhaps.

He took a tube of polyfilla and filled the crevice, but he slept fitfully. He dreamt that a giant harlequin sprawled across him, smothering him, suffocating him, infecting him. He woke, sweating. He threw himself under the shower; he turned the pressure higher and higher, but the water did not cleanse him.

At work, he could busy himself, focus on the telephone calls and meetings, but he could feel the nightmare squirming - heaving like the sea - beneath his feet, trying to break free. He didn't stop when he got home – he cleaned his car, he cleared a garden shed that had not been cleared in decades, he dug a patch of vegetable garden.

'Christ,' he gasped when, finally, he forced himself to enter the bathroom.

The left-hand wall of the window cavity was black – Euston Station at rush hour, a rustling and bustling of thousands of commuters. The ladybirds were spreading, slowly and inevitably, around the window frame, the polyfilla breached.

He fitted the suction tube to the dyson. Magically, the wall was clear again, but when he looked into the container, some lady birds were flying about. He took it out to the dustbin. He banged on the bottom to clear every last harlequin and, even as he did so, he felt the touch of tiny wings against his face. He slapped and swung and flailed at them but all he caught was air.

He glanced upwards as he brushed his teeth. A harlequin crawled through the crevice. He carried the image of it to his bedroom. Every little creak of the timbers, every groan of the pipes, every breath of the wind, he imagined them.

He imagined them breaking out of the bathroom, crawling silently along the passageway and into the bedroom. Every little touch of his pyjamas, every little itch of his body, he imagined them. He scratched at his arms, his legs, his shins, his cheeks, his neck. They're in my bed, he thought. He turned on the light. There was nothing. No ladybirds. No sounds.

And then… a harlequin fluttered across the room,

unconcerned, and landed on the lampshade, inches from his head.

"Bastard!"

He went to the cupboard where the insect repellent lay. Fiercely, he sprayed his bedroom until he was almost asphyxiated. He smothered his body with the gel. He tried to sleep again. In the greys and dark greys and light greys and black of his sleeplessness, a shadow caught his eye.

Above the curtain.

They were in the room. A giant cluster of them seethed across the rail. Some were climbing down the curtain, closer to his bed. He screamed. He aimed the spray at them and some fell, writhing, to the carpet.

He took the gel and smeared it, in great globs, around the legs of the bed. He climbed back under the covers, wrapping the duvet tightly around him. He closed his eyes. He could hear the faintest rustling, like the wind brushing through the leaves of a tree before a storm.

He turned over. For a few minutes, he forced himself to stay still. But it was too much. All he could picture, in the blackness, was an army of harlequins marching, determined, across the carpet and up the bed legs. Some fell by the wayside, overcome by the fumes and the gel, but, like an invading army, others behind marched over the dead bodies of their comrades, advancing up the sheets to his pillow. He threw back the covers and, without looking back, ran downstairs to the living-room sofa.

In the bleary morning, he studied the carnage. A pile of harlequins lay on the carpet beneath the window – a pile big enough to scoop up with a shovel. More stuck to the curtain, which hung limp, discoloured by the spray. A few had made it further and lay now in the gel at the foot of his bed. A strange odour lingered in the room like stale nail polish remover.

He put on yellow marigold gloves and, holding his head back, vacuumed the curtain. He studied the corpses. The tiny yellow spots were on many of them. He turned the pile with a knife. They crackled slightly, like confetti or dried leaves.

He got to his office early that day. "Are you all right?" asked his boss. "You seem troubled."

"I could not sleep," he muttered and said no more.

He threw himself into his work. He took on his colleagues' work and when it was time to finish he went on working. He tried to stop, but the moment he stopped, the harlequins crept through the crevice in his mind.

They crept through, one or two at a time. He picked up his work again, threw himself at anything, picked up a brush and swept and swept, trying to sweep them away, but every time he stopped there were more of them. They crawled and swirled and wormed through his head and all he could hear was the cacophony of their wings and a yellow fungus was growing and bloating inside him, taking root like a cancer.

He ran to his car. He hammered his brow so hard against the steering wheel that momentarily it cleared his mind. He drove and drove, but he didn't drive home. He drove to another county. He drove to another part of his mind. He drove to his sister's grave.

He sat cross-legged, his face in his hands in front of it, overgrown though it was by a rose that they had planted at the time of her death.

"I'm sorry," he said, "I'm sorry, I'm sorry, I'm sorry."

'Be good to your sister. Look after her. Make your peace with her.'

His mother's last words to him surfaced from the swamp. She never knew either.

He stayed silent for some minutes. He could hear the

notes of a song thrush delivered, precisely, on the chestnut above him. He listened, and eventually he realised he was listening. He thought he was well enough to drive home.

He opened the front door. The house was clear. The bedroom was clear. The bathroom was clear. He ran a bath. For the first time in days, he relaxed. Expiation. He lay back and opened his book where he had left off.

His neighbour started a cordless drill. Strange time, he thought.

The sound circled, came closer. A huge moth burst through the bathroom window, whirring, as large as a humming bird. It flung itself towards the light and the walls of its gaol. Concussed, it fell to the floor. I'll chuck the body out later, he thought. But the whirring sounded again. It rose in a fury of wings and antennae, crashing and criss-crossing the room. Slowly but irrevocably it moved closer to the bath.

He held his hands out, ready. But the final kamikaze dive still caught him off guard. A wall of water overflowed the sides as he lurched out of the thing's way. For a moment it floated, still. He thrust forward, scooping his hands underneath and hurled it out. It must surely have drowned, he thought, but the soaked patch of carpet betrayed a copper-black outline, sticky, more than two inches long, that shook and moved. A beetle, a flying beetle. Not a moth.

He grabbed at it with a towel; he could feel the wings still trying to thrash. He stamped on it again and again until it dissolved into pulp, but, even as he did so, he heard the whirring again, beating, even louder now.

He looked out. Entire squadrons of the beetles, the last of the sun glinting off their glutinous wings, were bearing down on the house. He slammed the casement shut, but already they were hammering against the doors and window panes and roof tiles.

3 HUNGRY GODS

It turned out that we all thought the same thing as we neared the crater. When we talked about it afterwards. It was like Sam and Frodo's final climb - slipping, clutching and stumbling their way up Mount Doom to the summit of Mordor

But I get ahead of myself…

We gathered under the orange Four Winds sign at the airport. The man holding it said his name was Raoul. He was late twenties, tall, lean and good-looking with Rastafarian hair. Tired and jet-lagged, I stepped out of the terminal into the afternoon heat and clambered into the mini bus. People were beginning to nod off by the time Raoul stood up.

"Welcome to Nicaragua," he said. "I am going to be your guide and tour leader for the next week. We'll be walking in the mornings with early starts – the sun is too hot later. There are some challenges ahead but, tonight, chill out and enjoy the beautiful city of Leon."

A woman with cropped blonde hair and a strident

voice was outside as we arrived at the hotel.

"Anyone would think this was a bunch of pensioners, not a walking group," she exclaimed as we tumbled off the bus. I thought she must be part of Four Winds at first. Her face was set in a toothy and rather supercilious grin. Tilly was her name.

We sat down to dinner in random order.

"I'm Alex," I said, holding out my hand to the couple opposite as some wine appeared. "And this is my wife Paula."

"Martin and Ruth."

"So where are you from?" I asked, though it was fairly obvious from their accent.

Ruth had barely started to describe their home in Masham, North Yorkshire before Tilly butted in.

"Masham," she said, mashing the name of the picturesque market town like a potato, "is a pretty dead-end place, isn't it?"

"It's Mas-ham, and it's not…" started Ruth, who was barely five feet tall and looked as timid as a mouse. But she was cowed into silence by the onslaught of Tilly's words. I forget everything the woman went on to say. It is not important. Not to what happened later.

I could feel Paula bristling beside me but Tilly was already telling someone else how things were. It seemed that she worked for some advanced software company. Perhaps she was highly intelligent, but she had all the social skills of a Windows operating system. I noticed that Ruth did not speak a further word to her, nor would turn in her direction.

We gathered at 8.30 a.m. for each day's walk, loaded like pack horses with water. Tilly would stride ahead commando-style in tight shorts that might have suited someone half her age.

"It's not a competition," she said every morning.

It was probably the third night that she became officially an unwelcome member of the group. Seated on the landing on our floor of the hotel after most of us had turned in, we could hear her clearly. At first, it was general criticism of Four Winds; then I heard my name mentioned; and then, in a mimicked Yorkshire accent, she was talking about 'little tubby marshmallow'.

I opened the bedroom door. Tilly was sprawled across a sofa, beer bottle in hand. Ed, her thick-skinned husband, lay to her left, virtually comatose until I spoke.

"Tilly, we can hear every word you say out here and we're trying to get some sleep. If you want to criticise me, then bloody well do so to my face. And if you're not happy with other people in the group either, then I suggest you leave."

She did not say anything but stood up. As they left, Ed turned and murmured an apology quietly in my direction.

The evening before the Telica climb was the fish restaurant in Las Penitas on the coast. Make your own way there, taxis back, Raoul had said. Paula and I clambered onto a bus, one of those big yellow American school buses that you see on 1960's videos. Wide-smiling Nicaraguans together with American and Dutch back-packers, some with surf boards, were our fellow travellers. Flame-red malinche trees, blue magpies and malnourished horses lined our route.

The group's resident bachelor, Philip, was seated at one of the small tables at the restaurant, already several sheets to the wind, when we got there. He waved vaguely towards the vacant chairs. A spectacular sunset was forming, surfers backlit on the sand, and I saw Martin and Ruth making a beeline for us. Ruth slumped in a chair.

"Thank God we don't have to sit with that woman."

She paused. "And thank you for saying what you said last night."

Telica is a challenging climb, Raoul had said. It is a seven kilometre ascent to the rim of the volcano. There are sustained steep and difficult sections. There is no obligation to go. The original schedule had included the moderate climb to El Hoyo, part of which was on horseback. But El Hoyo was closed because it had become active again.

Only Anna, a Dutch lawyer, dropped out. No-one thought the worse of her and later, of course, no blame could be attached to her. She was the only one not to be questioned.

At six the next morning, we embarked in three 4x4's. We could see Telica in the distance. It looked high, barren and, to me, cold and forbidding.

Suddenly the jeep took a turn off the highway, doubled back on itself under the road and we were bumping along a rock-strewn track. Eventually, we pulled into an open area. Raoul came to each jeep – water, more water, sunblock, insect repellent. We set off uphill and before long I was building up a sweat.

"Feeling the pace are we Alex?" I heard the voice behind me as we climbed a steep rocky path, the mountain to one side and a precipice to the other.

'I could just push the bloody woman off' - I do not deny that the thought crossed my mind.

We stopped under the shade of a large mango tree for a snack.

"After this it gets more difficult," said Raoul. "It will take us about two hours to the top from here."

I tried to block out this information. The volcano still looked miles away and I was already tired. I glanced at Paula. She rolled her eyes as we heard Tilly's voice yet again from behind a bush.

"You want to hold on to some of that water, Ruth. You'll need it at the top."

She appeared.

"Ready Paula? Got your suncream on?"

Something snapped in me.

"For Christ's sake, Tilly, they're not schoolkids."

Ed winked at me. "Well said," he said.

She shut up for a moment and walked off following Raoul's lead. Everyone dropped back some yards behind her. Her lurid yellow jacket, bobbing in front, made me think of a traffic cop at the scene of an accident.

The track became steeper and steeper, footholds insecure amongst the loose stones. I could hear my companions' breathing becoming louder in front of me and behind me. The lactic acid was building in my thighs and I had to will my legs to carry on upwards. We stopped briefly to watch two electric-blue morpho butterflies dancing in the bush. My heart was pounding and still the volcano looked miles away, daunting, wild and untenanted.

Philip was gasping for breath. 'What the hell do we do if he has a heart attack?' I speculated idly to myself.

Somehow we went on and magically the path flattened out for a while.

Raoul pointed ahead. "This is the last hike," he said.

One final step and there suddenly ahead was Telica like a massive breaking wave, its far rim, on the opposite side of the crater, poised above us. Colour and all forms of life and growth ran out here on the desolate steep scree that led up to the edge of the crater. The wind howled through a cold drizzle

Ruth bent down to tighten her boot laces.

"What you need to do is cross them over the last hook first and then back to the second last," said Tilly. A stifled cry, explosion almost, of indignation emitted from Ruth as she moved away from the woman.

"Patronising bitch," she muttered under her breath. And then we started on the final Mount Doom climb.

Stones falling and feet slipping, we struggled up this bare ungodly landscape to the very rim of the volcano. Yellow impenetrable steam hung over the crater like fog and the acrid smell of sulphur hit me in waves. To the right, the rim curved round in a moonscape plateau before rising sheer and inaccessible. No fence held us back, no signs, nothing. We were at the very elemental edge of the earth.

The roar of the magma, the occasional glow of fire through the mist deep below, the towering wall of the crater opposite – it was too much for me and I turned my back, dizzy with vertigo and some other unnamed fear.

I glanced over to Paula. She was lying on her stomach, her long auburn hair hanging over the very edge of the crater. I shouted to her that she was too close, but she waved me away with a smile.

She nearly let herself roll over, she told me later. "It was so beautiful. It was almost as if Mother Earth was saying 'Come Home.' "

"While you can still hear me," shouted Raoul above the roar, "I want to tell you..." He pointed with his arms North-West and South-East. "Right here we are on the line of the CAVA, the Central American Volcanic Arc, which runs all the way from Guatemala to Costa Rica. The furthest volcano to the north in Nicaragua is Cosiguina, and then there is San Cristobal, the highest, that you saw on the way out of Leon. To the south are thirteen more – including Masaya, and Concepcion on Ometepe Island in Lake Nicaragua. OK, relax for a while - we'll chill out here for thirty minutes."

He sat down, nonchalantly opening a pack of peanuts.

Gesturing to Paula, I moved fifty metres or more away to a large lava rock. I felt calmer there, and surveyed the fertile valley below. I looked back. I saw Paula's rucksack sitting, alone and untended, close to the volcano's edge. My stomach lurched … and then I saw her sauntering back.

I pulled out my camera and took a few shots. The turquoise of the rucksack and her luminous green top stood in dramatic contrast to the side of the crater swirling in and out of view behind her.

******

From this point on, I can only relate what she told me. Paula is an artist. She notices things. Her word is all I have to go on. To piece together what happened.

Still sitting on the edge of the crater, she had noticed Tilly heading off to the right, dipping over a contour and out of sight. She remembered laying a half-eaten bag of crisps on the stones between herself and the crater. Suddenly the wind had picked up and swept away the crisps. She had lunged for them, then realised it was a lost cause and let the bag sail out over the edge and into the burning cauldron.

She had noticed Philip, still gasping for air and muttering to himself. She had noticed Martin busily unpacking his rucksack, the rucksack that we had admired over the days for its abundance and efficiency. She had seen Ruth donning a scarlet rain jacket, one of its treasures, and then heading off like a mobile pillar box.

"I could see everyone," she said. "Some people were engrossed in their mobiles, others were taking photos or just eating their snacks and looking out at the volcano –

what you'd expect. At one point, I could hear stones being thrown in the air by the magma at the bottom – just for a few seconds…And then Ruth came back. She went straight to Martin, and collapsed in his arms. They spoke for a while and he caressed her hair. Martin went across to Raoul who called Ed over."

"…trying to climb the high … couldn't see anything … thought she heard a …," was all Paula had been able to hear.

She had seen Ed pull out his mobile and tap the screen, then, after a few moments, screw up his face.

"Please, everyone - do not move," Raoul had said, and headed off into the mist with Ed.

******

Disembodied cries of "Tilly, Tilly," echoed round the mountain, somehow audible above the grumbling of the volcano, as I rejoined the group. People were looking at each other. Raoul and Ed returned, trickles of blood seeping from grazes on their hands and knees and a grim look on their faces.

"Tilly is missing. Ruth says she heard a scream," said Raoul, his voice faltering. "She may have fallen and hurt herself. We have to search where we can. Please…stay close together."

We fanned across the scree, scrambling to reach a higher level, Raoul taking up position closest to the crater. The stench of sulphur became stronger and the mist thicker with every step. Perhaps we knew that there was no joy and no hope in this exercise, and by the time we had re-grouped all were silent and exhausted. Raoul called a number on his mobile and spoke urgently in Spanish.

The journey down seemed to take forever. We had

been twelve going up and we were only eleven coming down. Ed was silent. A doubt, a suspicion, an uncertainty, a kind of guilt hung over the group.

We met a member of the Policia Nacional and a paramedic, carrying a stretcher, on their way up. Raoul talked to them, gesturing to Telica, ourselves and the heavens as if imprecating some higher law. We stopped at the same mango tree to eat, but the food tasted empty and when we finally reached the bottom, a police 4x4 and an ambulance were waiting along with our own vehicles.

"They want statements from everyone back in Leon," said Raoul, "but they want all the cameras now..."

Reluctantly, we handed them over. We looked at each other as we drove back. Did we simply say what we had witnessed on the mountain, or did we elaborate on the background to the week? Did either make a difference?

The heat of the day lingered in the Leon police building, its magnificent colonial frontage giving way to a bland, dirty cream interior, cockroaches lurking on the walls. A fan turned from side to side in the ante-room as I handed over my passport and waited my turn. I tried to think about things from a police perspective. Someone was missing presumed dead, very possibly fallen into the volcano. That person had left the group and disappeared out of sight. Two other people had left the group and disappeared out of sight. Both of them had expressed frustration and dislike of the missing person. My position looked precarious and, as I entered the interview room, my assessment was confirmed by the cheerless glare of the two officers sitting under a portrait of Daniel Ortega. My camera lay on the desk in front of them.

I described my movements, but I could see that they did not believe me. Then they started flicking through my photos. One of them caught their eye – it was one that I had taken from the rock. They scrolled through the photos more slowly, blowing them up as they went.

"Ah," exclaimed the older of the two officers, squinting through his spectacles. I looked but could see nothing. His stubby finger pointed. I looked more closely and, way beyond Paula and her turquoise rucksack, a faint but defined yellow haze became visible at the far edge of the crater. He scrolled the image over to the left, and, just a few yards behind, a similar scarlet shape could be seen. I gasped and studied the picture again, trying to compute what I was looking at.

"You go," he said, flicking the memory stick out of the camera. "Back tomorrow."

Music was spilling out of the Hostel San Jose as we walked back. I was suddenly dying of thirst and longing for a cold lager.

"Dos cervezas por favor."

"Coming up," said the tall young man behind the bar, fresh, I guessed, from Exeter or Bristol University. The room was filled with backpackers, most of them deep in their iPhones, oblivious of the world around them.

An arm waved from the open courtyard behind and we walked across to find our entire group round a table. Raoul had not gone home, even Ed was there and Anna had found us. I slumped in a chair and took a long draught, physically stiff and mentally exhausted. Deep red lilies and winding purple clematis adorned the terrace. The walk, the volcano, everything that had happened seemed very far away, part of a dream. And yet the dream was the only thing we could talk or think about.

Anna adopted the role of attorney in this surreal courtroom. She asked each of us to tell her what we had seen and experienced. I explained about my visceral fear of Telica, Paula told how the volcano had drawn her in and so it progressed around the table. Jessie and Caroline were convinced that Ruth left before Tilly; Mark did not see either of them go but saw me go and then disappear out of sight. Ruth told her story again – was the noise she heard a scream or a cry? Against the noise of the bubbling magma, it was hard to define any sound, she said.

I did not mention the photograph – I was not judge nor jury.

Ed' s voice broke at times. "I may be some time," Tilly had called out as she got up and left. But she often said that sort of stuff, he said – he had not been worried.

I looked at Paula and around the table. Everyone was lost in their own thoughts, but no one wanted to be alone. 'Do you feel glad that you will not see this woman again, or just plain shocked at the apparent manner of her passing?' I wanted to ask them.

Someone had left a travel book on the table. I thumbed through it, something to engage my hands, my brain. The excerpt and footnote in the volcanoes section caught my eye and I glanced through it, then read it with more attention:

In the myth of the Chorotega Indians of Nicaragua, a woman was sacrificed to the god of the volcano when it was active. The chosen person was given 'chicha' (corn beer) and chocolate and then thrown into the volcano to propitiate the god's anger. Although we have not been able to find any written evidence of this, there is circumstantial evidence in the form of the petroglyphs around Masaya and on Ometepe island depicting a fierce monkey god emerging from a volcano and a figure and table on the rim of the crater.

Archaeologists have also found remains of human bones and an altar embedded in the lava flow.

Barber, J. (1985). *The Native Indians of Nicaragua and Costa Rica.* Atlantic City, New Jersey: Georgetown University Press. ISBN 0-8147-2857

A silence descended as the book was passed from one person to the next. Ruth handed it to Martin, her face expressionless. I wanted to protect Ed from reading it, but he was insistent and when he looked up, his hands were folded in a form of prayer.

.

4 COLD DARK STEEL

Cold,
Cold dark steel
A black disc rearing
On wooden wheel
Roaring
Its flaming breath
Ripping
Through trees
Smashing
Through barns
And village streets
Scything
Through ranks
Of serried men
And sodden uniforms
And tented officers
Then rearing
And roaring again

Days in the Life

5 HOME AGAIN

Home.

I stumble off the bus, its stale smells of diesel and people. I stand and breathe the air. Air salted with the fish and the nets of a thousand years. I dump my rucksack and stare at the sea, its rhythms alive in me. Rolling in, rolling out; whispering in, whispering out; storming in, storming out; breathing in, breathing out. Herring gulls wheel and shout above, my soundtrack.

The stuff – the lectures, the dissertation, the chatter of the iPhone, the flat mates, even Sarah – drains away from me like a heavy shower washes clean the night. Already, I wonder why I brought the books.

I walk the fifty yards, the fishing boats in the harbour to my right. I turn the corner and gasp, as I have always done. The street grabs me in my gut, hugs me, beckons me forward. It is more colourful than I can ever remember it – more colourful in honour of him. On days like these, when hard rain, that penetrates the space between the rooves, has fallen and the sun shines, it is like a stream in rippled flood.

But I know the games of this light. I climb firmly forwards across the old wet cobbles, towards my window. My window that arrows down the street to the sea. If I were in my room, I would see me now. What has been going on in there since I've been gone? Now that I am looking in, not out.

I pass the rusted pipes of Mrs Tremethick's house. Pigeons have been roosting on them and left their mark. I pass old Joe Curgenven's buoys and floats that adorn his railings like a maverick Christmas tree. I can hear him say, 'Where have you been boy? Will you come out with me in the morning and set the nets?' He calls it through the window before my thought finishes. And I nod. "I'll be there, Joe. After the day." This is where I belong.

I pass the balcony with the palm-tree sunshade. 'The London people's house', Mum and Dad always laughed. They did not calculate, the London people, how many hours of sunshine they would get on a tiny patio perched above this cart-wide way. I pass the lilac in Number 12, its fragrance mixed with the earthy blast of the geraniums below. Always flowers in the Number 12 garden.

I reach the powder blue walls and the unlatched door. 'Mum,' I shout, and I hear her footsteps tip-tapping over the tiles. I smell Dad in the fabric of the building, in the coats that hang at the foot of the stairs, and in those stairs, and in the chairs, and in the faded books that line the shelves and in the wood of them. We hug and sob together our bodies rising and falling like the waves.

I am glad that we can say goodbye to him in this church. This church that looks across the roof of the house and down this narrow street. Down this narrow street to the sea; and across the sea to the horizon.

6 ROWAN'S STORY

Fabian stood on a disc of green grass, a disc of blue sky, of the same size, above him. An old but well-oiled push mower leant against a tree alongside a folding garden chair, and an olive green bivouac tent was almost invisible beside them. When he peeked inside, he could see a camping gas stove, a kettle, a tin and two mugs.

The roundabout stood at one end of the old by-pass. Few people took this route these days unless they lived in the nearby farms and hamlets. If you were going somewhere else, you took the new motorway and if you were going into town, you took the town road.

It was not any old roundabout. It was a tall roundabout, stately, like a tea clipper in full sail, built probably in the '60's when Fabian was still a boy and town planners were designing garden cities. If it were in the middle of a field, you'd call it a copse or a spinney. It was really a set of concentric circles – a verge of grass, then a sprawling thick jungle of rhododendrons, laurel and potentilla and finally a ring of poplars growing straight and true to the sky. In the centre was a clearing, the grass, not surprisingly, mown.

"What the hell?" exclaimed Fabian out loud. Then, "Buddy - here, heel," addressing his dog, a chocolate brown labrador whose wild rush across the deserted road in search of a fleeing rabbit had brought him to this place. He looked around. There was no litter, and there were no further signs of human habitation. Not a tramp, he thought, nor a drug addict – too neat. Nor someone on the run - too much order. He wanted to know more.

Fabian was the son of Tristan Sopwith, a famous TV presenter of the Swinging Sixties. His childhood home had been adorned with photographs of his father with Mick Jagger, Twiggy and Jimi Hendrix and a pair of framed chelsea boots had hung in the hallway. There was a story behind them, but he had never really found out the full details. He suspected there was something of the Stones and the mars bar about them.

He had worked for the BBC himself, though never at the glorified heights his father had dreamt for him. He had produced historical documentaries – he loved the research and the investigation - and had later worked on the Panorama team with Natalie.

He thought he had come to terms with her death now. At the time, they had said she might have been saved if they could have got to her more quickly, if they could have got her out more quickly, and his mind had been wracked with if's…*if* the man who had found them had called 999 sooner, *if* he had taken the day off and driven her himself, *if* that idiot Ian had not been driving. But this was all ten years ago.

Now his life seemed to have filled itself with tennis, art classes, parish council meetings, gardening and shopping, a retirement schedule that was neither unpleasant nor demanding. Indeed, it brought to his mind the Pink Floyd song 'Comfortably Numb'. At times, however, he wondered whether there was not something more, some secret to life that he had not yet unlocked. In any event, it was not until the following Sunday that he was able to get back to the roundabout.

He parked in the entrance to a field a couple of hundred yards away and out of sight. Reconnaissance, he thought to himself, as he walked up the road, Buddy on a lead. He kept an eye out for birds bursting out of the bushes or unexpected sounds, but there was nothing. He made landfall on the verge without incident, then tunnelled his way through the laurel, his limbs protesting at the bending and twisting as Buddy hauled him forwards enthusiastically.

When he reached the clearing, he shook himself down and blinked in disbelief. A man was standing on his head fifteen yards away on the opposite side. His red t-shirt had flopped downwards, revealing a trim stomach. Buddy rushed up to him all pals and lolling tongues, then, perhaps a little confused by this upside down man, barked inquisitively. The man barely moved.

"Hello, boy," he said. "Where did you come from?

He caught sight of Fabian, lowered himself into a half headstand and, with practised ease, righted himself.

" 'Afternoon," he said, spreading his arms wide. "Just spreading the blood around a bit. Welcome to the roundabout."

"We…er…came upon this place the other day, when Buddy started chasing something," said Fabian, inclining his head towards the dog. "I was intrigued to know who lived here."

"Oh, I don't live here," said the man in a gentle West Country burr. "It's my retreat, my garden, but I hold no dominion over it. It is not mine. Cup of tea?"

"Thanks," said Fabian, head spinning. This encounter did not fit into the normal framework of his life.

"I've got two mugs in case anyone ever came, but only one chair, I'm afraid. But the grass should be pretty dry today."

Fabian took the large enamel mug. The man had thrown in a couple of teaspoons of sugar without asking, but he took a sip and the taste was good.

"I'm Fabian…or Fabe."

"Tommy. Great to have a visitor. "

"So why here, what brought you here?"

"It's pretty straightforward. I have a flat in town, it's nice enough but there's no garden. Thing is, I've always loved wildness, and you don't get that from a window box. I'm a bit tight on money, so buying somewhere out in the country is beyond me. I tried the Lower Park. It's nice enough, but you can't get away from the schoolkids swearing and smoking everywhere and the drunks and… so I started looking around outside town. Then I came across this place. I don't know who it belongs to – the council, I suppose. And I think that means me in some tiny part, and you. So I thought, I'll try it, see if anyone objects."

"And how long has that been?" asked Fabian, noticing suddenly that a flowerpot had been laid into the turf in the centre of the clearing.

"First came here last August," said Tommy. "So nearly a year. Never seen a soul before you. I just come here and do some yoga, or read or just watch the world go by. Not the outside world, but the roundabout world. You would not believe how much goes on here."

Fabian waited for a minute as an unusually noisy vehicle, probably a tractor, circumnavigated the roundabout, the driver no doubt blissfully unaware of the life within it.

"And the flowerpot hole?"

"Ah…when I need to stretch the limbs, I put in a bit of cross country clock golf. Twenty-nine is the record, but I managed a flukey hole-in-one that day."

Fabian smiled, stretched and lay down on the dry earth, pungent with the smell of cut grass and rotten leaves. Something about the illogicality of the place, the non-conformity of the man, spelt freedom to him. He watched a black stag beetle crawling up a blade of grass, then looked up at the disc of sky and the patterns in the wispy clouds above him. A man smoking a long pipe lingered for a while, then merged into a crocodile. He felt no urge to speak or to leave. He did not know if he had been lying there for five minutes or thirty when Buddy suddenly started barking at the clackering of a magpie and his reverie was broken.

"I must go. Buddy, come on boy," he said. "Mind if I come back?"

"Of course," said Tommy. "All yours."

On the turn-off towards his home, a hand-drawn sign announced 'PARTY', an arrow pointing. He thought nothing of it until he noticed black, white and red shapes in the distance. For a while, his eyes could not make out what he was seeing. And then he realised it was Mickey Mouse, a very tall lanky Micky Mouse, along with Minnie Mouse, standing on the edge of a field.

Mickey waved him down and Fabian came to a stop. A girl – or was she a young woman - popped out from the hedge somewhere behind Mickey.

"Are you coming to the party?"

"No, I live in the village."

"Ah well," she said, "Sorry to have bothered you."

She had a wonderful smile. She reminded him of

Natalie when they first met in the students union.

A couple of minutes later, he was home. For a moment, he sat in the car and closed his eyes. He let his jaw relax and shook his head quite violently from side to side. Had it all been a dream? Had he lost his marbles or taken the wrong pills? But nothing had changed and he felt excited, elated, as if some of the shackles of his life were falling away.

******

When Fabian returned to the roundabout the next day, Tommy was standing over a putter.

"Greetings," he said, handing him a golf ball. "Winner takes all."

"All what?"

"All the glory."

The hours were marked by a pile of fir cones, each hour one point five long Tommy-strides from the next around the circumference of the disc.

Fabian started on the one and aimed for the sunken flowerpot. The ball veered off to the left, snatched by some unseen golf goblin. Tommy's ball was straighter, then snagged in the newly-cut grass. Fabian studied the lie of the land. How difficult could this be? He addressed his ball firmly. It was heading straight towards the hole and his fist was already raised in a triumphal 'Yesss', when it curled around the lip and faltered to a standstill.

Tommy laughed.

"I do my best with the mowing," he said, "but St Andrews it is not."

It was past five when the girl emerged from the bushes. A wire hung from her left ear and she had a stud in her nose. She wore combat trousers and carried a light rucksack. Shock registered on her face as she surveyed the scene.

"Hello," said Tommy and Fabian, almost in unison

For a moment, she looked as if she might turn and run, but she took the ear-bud out.

"Hello," she said weakly. "I…er, sorry, just looking for some peace and quiet."

"No apology necessary," said Tommy. "You've come to the right place. Cup of tea?"

Clearly, thought Fabian, while Tommy's approach to rural living was somewhat eccentric, his idea of hospitality was very British.

"Thank you."

She sipped in silence for a while.

"I was trying to do some writing," she said. "Couldn't focus at home. Too much going on."

Tommy offered her the seat.

"I'm Tommy, this is Fabe. We've been roundabout friends for all of two days."

Fabian looked at her, guessed she was mid-twenties. He nodded towards her.

"And you are?"

"Rowan."

"Nice name. So what are you writing?"

"Oh, I don't know. I suppose it's a poem though it might turn into a story."

"Are we allowed to hear any of it?"

Rowan sipped her tea, then looked out at the trees.

"OK, the first two lines. Here goes…" she took a deep breath.

" *Let us suppose the mirror broke,*
Would the window then look out?' "

"Mmmm…," said Fabian after a while. "There's a whole world in that question."

Tommy nodded.

Rowan leant back and closed her eyes. Fabian lay on the ground in his newly found cloud-observation posture, and Tommy sat cross-legged, his back against a tree..

"How do I know you guys aren't weird?" asked Rowan suddenly. "For all I know, you might rape me and bury me here, never to be found again."

"Well, yes, I suppose so. But how do I know that you and Fabian won't attack me and eat me alive?"

Rowan giggled.

"I'm a vegetarian. "

"I promise I won't rape you and bury you, if you promise not to eat me alive."

"Cool," she said, and with that word an unwritten bond was formed between the three of them.

"You know what," said Fabian. "I think we need some rules for this place."

"Rules? Why do we need rules?"

"Well, you know, like No Facebook or No Litter."

"Ah, OK, I'll second those."

"No Swearing."

"Keep the roundabout a secret between the three of us."

"Any more?"

"No Mobiles."

"Agreed?"

All nodded. And so the rules of the place were set.

******

The summer passed in a wave of roundabout time. Fabian found himself, in his ordinary life, dreaming of being back in the roundabout. Sometimes he would go there and find he was alone. Sometimes Tommy would be there meditating and Fabian would be quiet until he was done; sometimes Rowan was there or both of them. Sometimes one of them would bring a bottle of wine and a simple meal. They would heat it, if it needed heating, on the camping gas stove and sit in a circle on the grass eating and the act of sitting together felt like a form of prayer.

Fabian had begun to take along his easel. He knew he had no great talent as an artist, but he liked to brandish his brush across the canvas like the conductor of some grand orchestra. Sometimes, however, he simply put the brush down and watched and listened as the roundabout world moved around him in a form of parallel time.

"Want a go?" he had asked Rowan one time, offering her a clean canvas and a brush, but she'd shaken her head.

"If you could see how I draw, you'd understand," she had said. "I can't even draw a stick insect. I try to paint a picture with my words instead."

She had started to bring along a ring-bound pad, and scribbled voluminously in it.

"What are you writing now?" Fabian asked.

"It's a story about two men who live on a roundabout," she said.

He laughed.

"Let me guess their names. Can I read it?"

"When it's finished."

"Have you worked out an ending? They always say the ending is the most difficult bit."

"Not yet."

Tommy appeared one day in a sweat shirt that read, 'We believe one family torn apart by war is too many."

"It's a UNHCR slogan," he said when they asked him. "I worked for them and Medecins Sans Frontieres for thirty-five years."

Fabian and Rowan looked at him, understanding.

"It doesn't matter the country, so many countries," he said. "It was always the mothers that got me – the mothers whose husbands and sons had been rounded up and taken away, the mothers whose children had no food, their stomachs distended and their bones sticking out at awful angles, the mothers forced to leave their own land and live in a camp because of someone else's war, and the mothers who had to bury their children after ebola or some other outbreak."

******

It was in the early days of September that Rowan told them she was going back to university in two weeks. She wanted to have a celebration, a roundabout party before she left. Fabian felt a sense almost of grief, but they decided on the following Saturday.

"I have to be at our village fete first," he said. "They moved it back this year, heaven knows why. I'm supposed to be a clown, jollying everyone along to spend all their money. But I'll be here as soon as it's over."

Rowan and Tommy had been there some time and the light was already fading when a rustling in the bushes heralded the arrival of a figure in a three-quarter-length crimson braided jacket and lime green trousers. His face was painted red, eyes daubed in pale blue, brows high and white on his forehead.

"Sorry I'm late," called Fabian. "Damn judging went on for ever. Nowhere to change."

He subsided to the ground, his back against a tree.

"I wouldn't have known it was you, if I didn't know it was you," said Rowan.

She handed him a glass of wine, then picked up a flute. She played a few notes. Fabian vaguely recognized   the tune, something that Annie Lennox had once sung.

"You going to be OK – I mean, at university?" asked Tommy.

"Hope so," she said. "Will you be here if I need you?"

"Not planning to go anywhere."

Two eyes glinted momentarily in the trees.

"Fox," said Tommy. "He's done the kamikaze run across the road."

A full moon had risen to one edge of the night sky above the roundabout and everything glowed in a blueish light.

Rowan launched into Lord of the Dance. She played it quietly and then she sang it.

"*Dance, dance, wherever you may be, I am the Lord of the Dance said he.*"

Her voice was soft and powerful, an angel in the trees. Fabian and Tommy watched her, mesmerised. She picked up the flute again and danced as she played.

A car roared into the roundabout – an old car, thought Fabian, a blown exhaust, going too fast. He could picture the driver wrestling with the wheel.

Rowan stopped.

"Sounds angry," she said, echoing his thoughts.

The noise faded into the distance and she resumed:

'*I danced in the morning when the world was young, I danced in the moon and the stars and the sun…*'

Fabian and Tommy, man and clown, were both on their feet. Like demented puppets controlled by some heavenly source, unfettered by any earthly self-consciousness, their limbs moved in time and they swayed in a form of ghostly ecstasy.

Suddenly, they stopped as one. The car was coming back towards them. Its roar became louder and louder – no hint of braking. The driver seemed oblivious of the roundabout. They stood in mid-dance, frozen in time, and held their breath

Then, inevitably, the squealing of brakes, tyres screaming across the tarmac. A split second of silence, and a car reared into view, its headlights searching the sky, crashing through the rhododendrons like a charging elephant until a frightful, sickening crump against a tree. Its lights flickered for a moment, then went out and there was nothing.

They raced towards the wreckage. The car was bent like a banana and buried back-first in the bushes. Smoke and steam poured from it and the smell of leaking petrol was already in the air. In the half light, they could see the shape of a man sprawled across the bushes. He was bleeding profusely from his head.

"Rowan get your car. Get some light on here. Call 999," said Tommy, taking charge.

He knelt down to check the man.

"Can you get his legs, Fabe?"

They lifted him to the other side of the clearing.

"See if there is anyone else in the car." Something lurched in Fabian's gut. He grabbed a torch from the tent and parted obstinate branches to peer inside.

"Shit," he breathed.

Someone was in the passenger seat, a woman, her head slumped. Alive or dead he did not know, but he knew he did not have much time.

"There's a passenger," he shouted.

"Can you get them?"

Light poured on the scene as Rowan positioned her car on the verge, headlights on. A mess of branches stuck through the car at every angle. The driver door was partially open.

"Bloody doors are jammed."

They could hear something dripping.

"Get the putter," shouted Tommy, tending now urgently to the man.

Fabian understood and ran for the putter. He raised it high and smashed it against the windscreen. Glass sprayed onto the inert body. In a kind of daze he realised it was the Mickey Mouse woman. Blood was dripping from her mouth and he redoubled his efforts.

He smashed against the windscreen harder. Again and again. The smell of petrol became stronger and stronger. Get out before the fuel tank goes up, a voice was telling him. But the woman was still in there and he thought of Natalie. He tore off his clown jacket. He laid the thick crimson serge across the jagged bottom of the windscreen and leant inside.

The seat belt would not release.

"I need a knife," he shouted.

Rowan pulled a large penknife from deep in her trousers, opening the largest blade. Fabian ripped at the belt with a frenzy. Head and shoulders in the car, he grabbed the woman under the arms. He could feel the heat from the engine beneath him. She was not big, but she was a dead weight, her body slumped forward, blood dripping onto Fabian's shoulder.

"Get her out… or jump," cried Tommy urgently.

Fabian gave one last heave and she came up through the windscreen, her clothes and skin tearing on the branches and the broken glass. Rowan took her weight and carried her in a fireman's lift as Fabian staggered back, his arms and hands lacerated, his face bathed in sweat, blood and makeup running across his face.

A muffled explosion came from inside the car, then flames poured up and around the bonnet as they reached safety.

"I think she's still alive," said Rowan in a shocked whisper.

Sirens blared in the distance. An ambulance and paramedics arrived simultaneously and Rowan led them through the bushes. Blue lights flashed all around.

"We need a way out of here with stretchers … quickly," said one of the ambulance crew.

A policeman began hacking a path through the thick laurel and rhododendrons. Fabian glanced across at the car, its fire now ebbing. But the bushes on either side, tinder dry from the long hot summer, had caught.

"Watch the fire," he called.

"Fire brigade will be here soon," said one of the officers.

But they did not arrive and a night wind fanned the flames.

The woman was lifted out first, the paramedics stumbling through the broken bushes. The ambulance sped away, its siren blaring again. They came back for the man. They seemed to have more time and laid him in the back of the vehicle. Fabian could feel the heat on his face. A ring of fire was spreading around the bushes to left and right.

"I need everyone off the roundabout – now," commanded the officer, though they needed no prompting.

One of the trees went up. A pillar of smoke and flames leapt into the night sky. Tree after tree caught, exploding suddenly like crackling bursts of gunfire. A vortex of swirling, searing orange rose from the ground, the tea clipper adrift in a blazing sea. By the time the fire engines arrived, the entire roundabout was ablaze, a huge burning torch, molten ash falling all around and everything consumed.

Tommy, Fabian and Rowan stood in silence, arm in arm, on the other side of the bypass, scorched, bloodied and stunned. They watched like this for minutes on end. Tears streamed from Rowan's eyes.

"I guess that's how my story ends," she said.

Days in the Life

7 THE JOKER

Joe scanned the room, searching for clues. The bookshelves that covered the walls were impressive. He looked at the dog. He was not good on dogs but it seemed friendly enough, putting its right paw on his seated knee. 'NCD, ETL, DL, TLFK, LRW, SIELF' –that's all the ad. had said, plus a box number of course. No GSOH's or WLTM's or N/S's. No *'Attractive, slim late 30's – interests include reading, swimming, travelling, eating out, cosy nights in - looking for a soulmate,'* and the like.

The door opened and Lorna came in.

"Bollocks!" she exclaimed.

"What's up?"

"No, nothing," she replied. "That's the dog."

Ah right, he thought, this is not going to be any normal form of relationship, wherever it's going.

She handed him a cup of coffee and subsided into an armchair. It engulfed her in its cushions, though somehow she seemed able to keep her own cup level and upright.

"So…" said Joe airily.

"Yep. This is me. Here I live with Bollocks and Fitz."

"And who's Fitz?"

"The other dog. Or bitch, should I say."

"A bitch called Fitz?"

"Yeah well, come on, use your imagination – bit of rhyming slang."

This is very different to Nadya, thought Joe. He'd met Nadya on the internet. She was very beautiful, but she did not seem to have a separate being to his own. When her visa had run out he had refused to marry her and she had gone back to Indonesia.

******

Sitting in an Indian restaurant waiting for the date – if the date don't come, you get your kicks from staring at the restaurant wall – I am the eggman…

And then she'd come in. How could he describe her? Not beautiful in an English rose sense, but beautiful in a high cheek bones, thirty-eight year old beautiful, languid-smiling chic sense.

Trousers, little make-up, a turquoise scarf swathed around her neck, she had launched into a bottle of red without much ado. They'd talked about this and that - her the ridiculous charade of dating websites, him the girl who'd found a guru and was never the same. But she said he'd have to wait to figure out what the ad. meant.

They had not really touched when they'd parted, merely an acknowledgement, the barest brush on the shoulder; but her eyes said yes, I will see you again. He had invited her to a premiere but she had insisted on her house. This was his initiation.

"Want to go for a walk?"

He was a city boy. He was used to going to the cinema or the newest restaurant or an art gallery on a Saturday afternoon.

But 'That would be great," he said gamely.

"Well you can't go like that. I'll get you a coat and some wellies."

"Aren't you going to translate the ad. for me first?"

"All in good time. Anyway it's not difficult. They're not riddles. It's just me. "

"Well, just the first one – NCD?"

"Have a guess."

"National Car Distribution? No Chance for Dinosaurs?"

"The No is right. The C is for City."

" No City…"

"Dwellers. No City Dwellers."

Lorna nodded.

"I fall at the first hurdle then," said Joe, crestfallen.

She shook her head. "The student has the space to learn, so says Confucius," she said mysteriously.

"Did Confucius really say that? Sounds more like Yoda."

Before he knew what was happening, a huge barbour that seemed to drown him in its embrace was wrapped around him, and his brogues were swapped for a pair of old green wellingtons.

Lorna re-appeared looking as chic as before, but somehow prepared for battle with the weathers in designer boots and jacket. Excited behind her came Bollocks and Fitz. She unhooked the leads and they marched out of the back door. Joe was acutely aware that his wellies were cold and made a sort of squelching, squeaking noise each time he took a step – a testament, he felt, to his lack of confidence in the countryside.

Bollocks bounded around exuberantly, longing for the open fields where he could go chasing after rabbits, pheasants or plain thin air; but in the meantime decided that Joe was a friend of his mistress and so leapt up at his waist.

"Don't worry about him," said Lorna. "Labradors are about the friendliest dogs in the world."

The only problem was that neither Fitz nor Bollocks seemed terribly obedient and soon all hell broke loose as they headed in different directions. "I'll get Fitz," shouted Lorna. "You get Bollocks."

Joe picked up a stick and headed off down a path in the wood in the general direction that Bollocks had headed.

"Bollocks… here," he called, mimicking Lorna's cries for Fitz.

Then louder, "Bollocks, here," and as he did so, an elderly couple came round the bend of the track, looking at him oddly.

He beamed at them, trying to convey with his smile that this whole situation, the lost dog, let alone the name of the dog, had nothing to do with him. But it was too much to accomplish with facial expression alone and the couple passed on, probably muttering to themselves about people from the city.

"Bollocks," he shouted, exasperated. And then out of the undergrowth came Bollocks, panting and friendly. Joe didn't know what to do. He did not have the lead and Lorna was nowhere to be seen. He patted the dog tentatively on the shoulder.

"Lorna," he called out.

He heard a faint cry.

Bollocks went racing off into the forest in the general direction of the cry. He would disappear, then come running back and wait while he caught up. After fifteen minutes, Joe felt he was lost.

"Lorna," he called again, but there was no answering call. Perhaps Bollocks was leading him on some wild goose chase into the depths of the forest, never to be found again.

"Lorna," he shouted more loudly.

"Yes, I'm here."

She sounded closer and after another couple of legs through the woods and undergrowth he could hear Fitz coming to greet them.

The two dogs seemed to confer and discuss the situation, then moved ahead together, Joe following panting. They came out into a clearing, a stream across it.

Lorna was lying on the far bank of the stream, at the side of a large greenish log. She was massaging her ankle and texting at the same time.

"Where did you get to?"

Joe felt suddenly responsible for leaving her.

"I went after Bollocks like you asked me to."

"Oh, he'd have looked after himself. Anyway, you're going to have to help me up. I've twisted my bloody ankle."

Joe looked at her. She was on the far side of the stream and had clearly fallen off the slippery green log.

"Jump it," she said.

He walked back, then launched himself forward, taking heroic, Usain Bolt-like strides towards the stream. But as he approached the edge, the resolve left him and he ground to a halt.

Lorna burst out laughing.

"Just do it, man," she shouted, half in pain.

He went back a bit further this time. He set off, self-conscious, hearing his wellies squelching underneath him and feeling his lungs wheezing as he approached the edge.

Don't stop. Don't stop. Jump.

His stride pattern was all wrong and he took off a full metre too soon. He landed just short of the far bank, a huge splash ensuing and a cry from Lorna as the cold water engulfed her. He clutched at thistles and elder roots as he dragged himself up onto dry land, bedraggled and yet somehow proud of this city boy.

"You're going to have to give me the next clue after that," he said.

"ETL? — Extra-terrestrial lighting? Exotic taste in lettuce?"

"T is right. Think about the bookshelves."

"Taste in…Literature? Eclectic taste in literature?"

"Yes…you're soaking," she said, as he eased his arm around her shoulders and gently lifted her forwards and up.

Now she was upright, one long, slender leg firm, the other hooked behind her, oh so sexy in any other circumstances, her arm wrapped about him in the forest clearing.

They got to the road after half an hour, the dogs yapping all about them at their slow progress.

" So DL?" said Joe.

"That one's easy."

"Dogs? Dog Lover?"

Lorna nodded as a bright blue pick-up finally appeared.

"God, Tom, what took you so long?" said Lorna, easing herself by arse jumps along the front passenger bench. The dogs leapt in the back.

Tom, a swarthy young man with the ruddy cheeks and jovial laugh of a farmer, looked across at her.

"Casualty?"

He pressed a button on the steering wheel and the sound of an ambulance siren blared from the roof of the vehicle.

"No, just take me home," she said, laughing. "This is Joe."

"*Heyey Joe,*" sang Tom, "*Where you goin' with that gun in your hand?* Sorry, couldn't resist it. I rent her the cottage. Try to keep her in order."

Lorna made it back inside, her arms clasped again around Joe's shoulder.

"Don't get any ideas," she said, as she stopped to catch her breath. "No, we can't stand here."

"Why not?" asked Joe.

She pointed at a picture. Joe could not quite make it out but it reminded him of the Joker in a pack of cards.

"I'm just superstitious. It nearly killed Rufo, my ex, the guy I used to live with, stupid man."

"What happened?"

"He was trying to paint the ceiling above the stairs. He rigged up this thing from the landing across to where the stairs turn. A plank and a step-ladder to support it on the other end. It was OK when he tested it on the landing end, but when he got beyond the middle the weight was too much for the step ladder and it slid inwards. The whole thing collapsed. He went flying and dislodged the picture on the way down. The corner caught him on the face. It was a complete mess when I came in – Rufo unconscious, magnolia paint and blood everywhere , the step ladder and the picture on top of him. He was lucky to get away with a broken shoulder and concussion."

******

Days in the Life

Under strict instruction, Joe found a bottle of Chilean merlot from the rack and a large bag of frozen peas from the freezer. He carefully skirted the Joker. The bottle was opened and dispensed into two glasses; only then was he allowed to apply the pack of peas to Lorna's ankle.

He thought back to the ad. What had he learnt? No City Dwellers – she seemed to be cutting him some slack on this one. Eclectic Taste in Literature – he felt qualified. Dog Lover - well, Bollocks and Fitz seemed to like him and that was surely half the battle.

He remained intrigued. TLFK, LRW, SIELF to go.

"So…Confucius, he say, put me out of my misery. Can we go through the rest of the clues?"

"OK."

"TLFK – Taste in Literature for …Kids?"

"Last word is right."

"Ah, Too Late for Kids. I'm cool with that."

"LRW?" he went on, feeling buoyant. "Long Reign for William?"

Lorna drank from an air glass.

"Wine," he said. "Red Wine…Likes Red Wine?"

Another one ticked off.

"SIELF?"

"Self-indulgent effusion and loads of fun?"

She shook her head.

"Self-interested ecstasy in lovely female?"

"Close."

"E?"

"Eventually"

"She I'd…Someone I'd eventually like to…"

"Yup," she broke in.

"And how am I doing?"

She said nothing, but as Joe left that night her wide, unbroken blue eyes smiled as her lips brushed his cheek and he knew he would see Fitz and Bollocks and the Joker again.

Days in the Life

8 THE BOYS

The makeshift map was scrawn in pencil on a piece of cardboard torn from a wine box. On the front was printed 'Vino Prodomenico -Imbottigliata in Italia'.

On the back, the map showed lines and fields and curious oblongs. Some of these were marked – 'yor howse',' big hegge', 'pond', 'Mr Potters red barn'. And then there was a large grey scribbled-in area. 'Wood' it said and, in one corner, 'rusty plow'. Beside the 'rusty plow' was an arrow.

"That's where to meet me," Salter had said.

The two boys studied the map, nervous now. They went in at teatime and washed their hands in the scullery.

"Not like you to wash your grubby hands without being told to," barked Mrs Tomlinson.

They looked at each other. They didn't want her getting suspicious. They were on their best behaviour as they ate, hiding their giggles behind closed palms when she turned their way. They took their plates to the sink.

"Shall we feed the chickens, Mrs Tomlinson?" This was

all part of the plan.

"You can, boys," she said. "You know where the corn is. Three scoops at the top, two at the bottom."

"Yes, Mrs Tomlinson," they said in unison.

They put on their gumboots and their baggy tweed jackets rumpled with age and the dirt of a thousand games. They made their way round the back of the old stone outbuilding to the chicken feed bin. They were out of sight now. They fed the chickens and, with a final glance at the piece of cardboard, skipped behind the big hedge and ran along its length.

They could see the pond where the hedge broke, and beyond it Mr Potter's red barn. The barn was on a small rise and it was only when they reached it that they could see the wood.

"There," one of them shouted.

"Ssssh!"

The bare trees ahead of them were slowly stealing the orange orb of the sun, a sun that had not been strong enough, through the day, to melt the frosted ground under foot. Behind them a pale moon rose.

In the dying light, the rusty plough was hard to distinguish from the turned earth and, when they found it, no one was there. Their faces creased in disappointment. He'd said after tea, after tea on Tuesday. They leant against the arms of the plough, clutching their jackets tight around them, cold and apprehensive now.

There was a rustling in the wood behind them. Fingers tensed on the old metal.

'Ssssh.'

From a clump of holly and rhododendrons, on his hands and knees, twigs scraping through his hair, came Salter. He looked around him.

"There you are," he said. "I thought you were never coming. Come on – follow me."

Days in the Life

9 DEEP ENERGY TRANSFER

"There's a mismatch. There are more…"

The door closed and I didn't hear the end of the sentence, but the speaker was clearly worried.

It had all started a couple of months back when I had had an Orthohealth cyberlink session. I'd developed a few creaks and pains - some things weren't working as they used to - and Barbara had said I should get myself checked out, make sure there was nothing sinister.

The consultant did a full QXI scan. "No major problems," he said at the end. "Just age .You could always go for D.E.T."

"What on earth is that?"

"Have you not heard of it? Deep Energy Transfer. It's a way of renewing the body, doing away with the effects of the years."

"Sounds good to me," I said. "How do we go about it?"

"I will make you an appointment at your nearest clinic for an initial assessment. They will determine if you are a suitable candidate for the procedure."

Two weeks later I rode my arrowdrone to the address I'd been given. It was an imposing building, designed to match the architecture of 18th century London. Cosseted gardens rich with proto wildlife spread either side of the long drive. Unseen eyes swept me and the smoked glass door slid open.

"Please sit down," said the zone director. He pointed to a faux-leather armchair, wing-back, like the ones you see in early 20th century spy movies. "There are sensors in the cushion, back and arms," he said. He made small talk while he waited for the data to scan and load onto his HUD.

Eventually he nodded. "All is fine," he said. "We can offer you D.E.T. if you would like it. The cost is £50,000. How much do you know about the procedure?"

"Nothing really," I said. "Please tell me."

"D.E.T. was developed in the early 2020's by a man called Dr Been. It stands for Deep Energy Transfer. Essentially, we download your entire self, your you-ness, all your characteristics, your memories, your experiences, your emotions, your appearance, everything that is you, into a meta-form.

"We take your body, with its creaks and groans, its furry arteries, its failing sight and hearing, its irritable bowels, its creaking joints, and pour in the deep energy fluid, paying particular attention to the areas of most concern to you."

"Knees," I said.

"Yes, I can see that they are probably a bit painful."

"And eyes."

"Them too," he said. "We can also factor the fluid to the age you would like to return to. Do you have an idea of what age, what level of energy, you would choose?"

"Twenty," I said, without thinking.

He nodded.

"Yes," he said. "Many of our male clients give that answer."

"It is, of course, fine, but … are you married, Mr Lewis"

"Yes. Forty years and counting."

"Indeed," he said. "Congratulations. But for +20 DET's we always recommend that the wife also has DET. Err… you understand?"

"I'll have to talk to Barbara," I said. "Anyway, what happens once the energy transfer is done?

"We upload you back into your revitalised body, and away you go."

"Are you sure this is entirely safe?"

"We would not be offering it to you if it was not. It is fully approved by NICE (National Institute of Clinical Excellence). You can see our reviews on Cybertrust also – they are all six star."

He gave me some references of others who had had the treatment. I met one of them in a pub.

"Had a couple of them," the man said heartily. "Couldn't recommend it more. Had my first in '28 when the procedure was in its infancy. Felt like a young buck again. They always said it was good for fifteen years back then. Had the second the other day."

He did a cartwheel across the lawn and winked at a young lady who was staring at him .

"How do I look for 93? You judge."

That persuaded me and here I was post-download. Mismatch – the staff had a problem it seemed, but it wasn't my problem.

"May I join you?" I asked a group sitting on a verandah hung with violet wisteria. Swallowtail butterflies danced amongst the bushes and Moroccan bee-eaters called from the higher branches.

"Of course," said a woman, beckoning me to a seat. "We're all in the same boat here."

"What boat?" I asked, stupidly.

"Well, you know, the Old boat. Trying to run like hell, trying to dodge the bullets." She paused. "You must have been a good-looking man when you were younger."

A serving partner appeared. He wore shades and a tiny syn card flashed at his belt.

"Coriander gin on ice, please," I said. The price of the transfer included unlimited drinks. "Anyone else?"

"What's that on his belt?" I asked after he had set down the glasses.

"Meta-form optron," said one of the group. "Lets him see us. We are all in meta and we can see each other, but people in base form can't see us. Not till we're reunited with our bodies. Unless they have those optrons."

Soothing, mystic music played over the etherwaves. A young, powerful voice called out numbers. One by one my drinking mates stood, gave a thumbs up or a 'see you later' and headed back towards their bodies. The woman winked, and thought-pinged a note with her FBYT code.

I was left on my own. A man walked towards me. He was wearing a dark suit uniform and an optron. His laser ID indicated he was the manager of the clinic, but he looked uncomfortable.

"Mr Lewis?"

I nodded.

"We have encountered a minor technical issue in your D.E.T. and your body is not quite ready. I'm sure our meta-technicians will resolve the issue before too long and we will be able to re-inhabit you. However, in case it should involve an overnight stay, let me show you to our

VIP suite - entirely free of charge of course. I will ask the serving partner to come back – please avail yourself of anything you require. I will keep you informed of the situation."

If I did not have complete faith in OrthoHealth, who, after all, had resolved the world Ecoli scare and had led the way in mitigating the medical effects of global warming, I would have been worried. I ordered another coriander gin and asked the serving partner to put on a series of ether albums from my youth - Coldplay and the like.

As the sound of 'Fix You' began to play through the air, I went back to the arrowdrone. It responded, without question, to my nano-code. The download had been successful. All my faculties and memories were fully functional. I could have a bit of fun here, I thought.

I flew the quick hop over to a pub I'd noticed near the clinic when I had first visited. Quaintly, it was called The Pheasant, a bird they used to shoot and eat before the 'admonishments'. A young couple were chatting on the far side of the room as I walked in. The girl watched the door as I opened it, then looked back enquiringly at her drink.

"Coriander gin, please," I said, approaching the bar. (I admit that I am not adventurous when it comes to ordering drinks).

The bar tender was a tall man, barrel-chested. His dark hair and florid complexion belied an inscrutable exterior. He didn't blink. He set the drink down on the counter at the point where he guessed I was.

"How you payin', mate?"

"Thought-sensor," I said.

He tapped the numbers on the ecoplasma screen and I transferred the code.

"Hey Charlie," he called. "Got one of your meta-mates here."

A man came over from the far side of the bar. The young couple were looking left and right.

"Did you hear that voice?" said the young man.

"Yes," she said. "Where is he?"

"Listen."

"Hello, mate. Done a runner from the clinic?"

"That's a different person. This is weird. This place is haunted," the young man whispered.

"No, no," I said, "You don't understand. It's not haunted. I'm not a ghost, I'm from the local clinic. Just left my body behind there."

Wine glasses and salads flipped to the floor, a blood red pool forming quickly on the tiles, as the couple ran from their table.

"Whooooo… whooo," I crooned in my best ghostly voice as they reached the door.

"Cut that out, now," said the bar tender.

"Just a temporary hitch," I replied to the man called Charlie. "They said my body wasn't quite ready."

"Hmm," he said. "Did they say anything else?"

"Well, soon after my download, I heard someone say 'Mismatch'. They sounded worried."

"Yeah, they would be. Means they have more meta-forms than they have bodies. Happens sometimes. Twins or a DNA problem often enough. You have a twin, or any donor organs?"

"Ah, no twin, but a cornea from a road traffic accident."

"That's probably it. Still you'd think keeping a count of meta-forms and base-forms would be a simple thing, but those guys - not sure if they studied mathematics at school. Even then. Mostly, the morning shift figures out the mismatch, Pheasant customer back in own body by afternoon. I'm Charlie, pleased to meet you…"

I didn't hang around. I didn't think to ask why he was.

It was a great day for flying. I set the Orbonav to follow a kestrel. We hovered, motionless, then swooped and dived low over someone's garden. I heard a scream. 'It's out of control, there's no one in it.' I did a loop the loop for the hell of it.

I parked in the Arrow bay, next to Barbara's. Her friend Keira was with her.

"I think you should do it," Keira was saying. "I mean, if what it says in the cyber mail is right, he's going to be horny, super-horny. And if you're not up for it … well, he's going to be after the young ladies big time. And didn't I read that we, as women, can choose – in the transfer – whether we want to be able to have babies again. I mean, Babs, this is your moment!"

"I know," said Barbara. "Sounds amazing, doesn't it? I suppose I'm just a little nervous…"

I input my usual, and not very original, booom de de boom boom, boom boom sonar key and opened the front door.

"Hello darling, I'm back," I called.

I could hear her rushing through from the patio where they had been talking.

"Where are you?"

"Here. Oh, no don't worry. You won't be able to see me."

I tried to hug her, but she pushed me away, screaming. Keira came up behind her.

"Keira, please, let me explain."

She glared, somehow pinpointing me.

"They've killed him. It's his ghost!"

"No, no – it's me. Don't worry. Everythings's ok. There's been some technical problem at the clinic…they're just trying to relocate my body. You can call them."

Days in the Life

I could feel Barbara's eyes as she turned 360 degrees. Even with her back to me, I knew I was in trouble. I nipped back to the Arrow, but she was faster. She'd turned off the AE supply. I was stranded.

10 HUNGRY SAILS

Hungry sails
billow and pitch
across the bay
like swirling veils.
At the bustling quay,
soaring masts
and morticed timbers
rattle and creak
in the pelting wind
and searing rain
that peppers the eyes
and chills the soul.
A motley band
of huddled men
cower behind
ten score casks
of hidden victuals

and coils of rope
a python thick,
while sea gulls wheel
and screech
and dive
above them
on the salted air
that reeks of seaweed
and the stench that creeps
from the street behind.
Uncertain now, this motley gang,
their sodden doublets
breeched,
await their turn
to cross the sea
under hungry sails

11 WHITE MAN

Kallista watched as Mandida rode back into the yard on the young chestnut, her black skin gleaming in the light of the Zimbabwe morning. She was probably late twenties, maybe a businesswoman of some kind from her confident manner. Some might have thought her arrogant, but it was just a trick of her face. Her strong jaw and high cheekbones were imperious, but when she smiled those same bones rearranged themselves and there was an unquestioned beauty about her.

Her eyes held Kallista's as she passed over the reins and dismounted.

"What did you think?"

"He's wonderful. Very responsive. How much do you want for him?"

Something in her colonial upbringing told Kallista she should ask twenty-five thousand in this, Mugabe's, version of her beloved country, but she resisted.

"Twenty thousand U.S.," she replied.

Their eyes met in recognition - not just of a deal but

somehow also of a beginning.

"OK," said Mandida. "I'll get a vet to look him over."

With that she climbed into a gleaming white Toyota landcruiser , drove past the sign that read 'Chikuda Stables, Kallista Russell – Livery, Training and Riding Instruction' above the red outline of a horse, and headed off with a wave. Kallista contemplated her departure with the sense of impending movement in her zodiac. Who was this woman who rode like an angel?

She saddled up Sovereign for a lesson with Victoria, a spoilt eleven-year-old white brat.

"The blackies are riding too now, are they?" said Victoria's mother disdainfully.

Kallista made no comment. The remark did not shock her. It was the language of lazy, colonial prejudice. Heaven knows, it was a language that Kallista was more than familiar with, the language of her upbringing. She could slip into it like an old baggy sweater, unthinkingly, if she was not careful. But this was the new Zimbabwe – she was trying to meet its demands and all her clients were valuable to her.

That evening, sitting in her garden with a drink in the quiet after sunset, she wrestled with her conflicts. The last birds flew in silhouette across the sky and an unanswered image of Mandida lingered in her consciousness.

She was, people said, a very eligible woman. Now thirty-eight, she remained slim and attractive though her auburn hair had lost some of its colour. It was three years since she'd left Isaac. He was twenty-five years her senior and, though he gave her everything she needed, she had felt suffocated. And so one day she had climbed into her battered red pick-up with a suitcase of clothes and riding gear and headed off into the sunset.

Her cell phone rang and her heart jumped as she saw

the caller's name on the screen.

"Hi, this is Mandi,"

"Hi," said Kallista, her heart pounding, feeling like a schoolgirl caught spying on her crush.

"I'll bring the vet at three tomorrow, is that OK?"

"That's fine," said Kallista, trying to sound calm. "See you then."

******

She thought of her father. Of the day they had come to take the farm. She could remember his words – she had never seen him like it before. He was red with rage and held a loaded gun.

"These Zanu PF bastards are not going to steal our house and our land."

Anna, her sister, and their mother Jane were pleading with him.

"Daddy, don't go out and fight them. They will kill you. Remember what happened to Bill; remember what happened to the Macphersons."

They could see Mugabe's so-called 'vets' approaching down the track to the farm and across the fields. Kallista could still feel the visceral fear of that evening.

Her father looked back at his family, his wife and his daughters, tears now running down his face, moving towards the track with his twelve bore.

Some of the faithful farm staff were standing nearby, frightened, unarmed and helpless.

And then he stopped. He looked around to Jane.

"Have you got the deeds?"

Kallista's mother, ever the pragmatist, had seen the writing on the wall from a long way out. She had decided on the important documents – the title deeds, the wills, the share certificates, the bank information, the passports – and had secured them in a wallet.

She nodded.

"Everyone into the truck - now," commanded her father.

The girls barely had time to pick up even the small emergency bags they had packed. They raced to the landrover and slumped into the back seats, the engine already started.

He gunned the accelerator and set off up the drive, zig-zagging between the pot holes and the 'vets'. It was only when they reached Mvurwi itself that he let off a little.

"You all OK?" he'd asked.

Kallista pictured the scene when they got to Uncle Ted's in Harare. They sat in the garden in the light of the moon, her father nursing a glass of scotch, his head bowed. Her mother looked on silently, in shock.

"I'm a bloody coward," he said.

"No, Daddy, you're not a bloody coward," said Kallista, taking charge. "You just saved Mummy's life and my life and Anna's life – and your own."

He looked up.

"Daddy, if it had not happened tonight, it would have happened another day. There was no point in dying for that."

He nodded and then reached for her and when they hugged his whole body crumpled in tears, crying for the lost farm, crying for the saved family, crying for the unknown future.

Anna and Jane joined in the hug and when the tears were done they stood back and looked at each other.

Her father punched his hand, palm down, onto the garden table.

"We'll sort this out ," he said.

Jane laid her palm on top of his, then Kallista, then Anna.

They had looked up. Uncle Ted was smiling, beckoning them to eat.

******

Kallista saw two vehicles coming through the gate just after three. The vet was Pieter Vos, a South African she already knew. Somehow she had expected a black vet. She led the horse out and held him while Pieter looked in his mouth, felt down his legs and his tendons and inspected his feet.

"Can you trot him up for me?" he asked.

She led the horse up the yard at a trot, then back again, straight towards Pieter.

"Looks sound to me," he said, turning to Mandi.

"Thank you, Pieter," said Mandi, "Will you send me your bill?"

Pieter took this as his dismissal and drove off, leaving the two women on their own, Mandi smiling.

Two eagles spiralled lazily in the sky above the stables, their occasional calls a spine-chilling warning to their potential prey below.

"I'm happy," she said. "I have my own horse. What shall I call him?"

"In the yard, we call him Leonardo."

"Why?"

"Oh, I don't know. Titanic. He's a good-looking boy isn't he?"

Mandi laughed.

"I'll think about that one, but I have to pay you."

"Come round to the house and I'll give you the bank details," said Kallista.

Days in the Life

Her bungalow sat beside the yard, surrounded by a mauve, white and yellow jungle of flowers - crossberry , bougainvillea and honeysuckle . Two stable hands had finished mucking out and were emptying their barrows onto a large pile as they walked past. The earthy smell of the manure lingered in the fragrance of the honeysuckle.

Mandi said something to the men in Shona and they laughed as Kallista selected a key from the ring at her waist and unlocked the door.

"You lock the door even when you're here?" asked Mandi, amused surprise in her voice. "You don't trust black people?"

"Ah, habit I suppose. Some of the staff came from the farm. I'd trust them with my life."

Kallista led her inside.

"Tea?"

"I would love a cup of tea, or maybe a gin and tonic?" she said, mimicking an English accent and looking around.

The day's newspaper lay on the table. 'Go back to England – Mugabe tells Whites' blared the headline.

Underneath it read, "Don't they know where their ancestors came from? The British who are here should all go back to England. What is the problem? We now have aeroplanes which can take them back far quicker than the ships used by their ancestors."

Mandi inclined her head towards the newspaper.

"And what do you think of our president's latest pronouncement?"

Kallista sighed. "I think – I think I never came from England. I was born here. I have a Zimbabwe passport. This is my home. I live here. I don't want to go to England. There is nothing for me in England. He has no right to demand I go there."

"May I call you Kallista?"

"Of course. Or Sta. Some people call me Sta."

"Star, like 'movie star'?" asked Mandi.

"Yes, but no r and no movie."

"Kallista," mused Mandi, savouring the name like a fine wine. "I like it. Does it have a meaning?"

Kallista laughed, self-deprecatingly.

"Actually, yes. It is the Greek for 'most beautiful'. In Greek mythology supposedly Zeus fell in love with a nymph named Kallista and, when his wife Hera found out, she was jealous and transformed her into a she-bear. And then Zeus hurled the she-bear into the heavens to protect her from being hunted and she became the Great Bear constellation. Something like that."

"Wow. But I'm going to call you Sta."

"And you," Sta went on, "where did you learn to ride so well? Tell me about you. "

"South Africa," she said. "We have a house there. My dad."

"And Mandida? What does Mandida mean?"

"You have loved me," she said evenly, levelling her eyes on Sta's.

She did not seem to want to talk any more about herself.

"Most beautiful…" she went on. "But does the she-bear have any he-bears? Don't you get lonely here? Do you have a family?"

Sta was busy with the kettle, suddenly aware that the room had filled with Mandi's scent, a sensuous concoction she recognised as Jo Malone's lime and mandarin. She felt a little light-headed.

"No, no family here. Plenty of friends. And the horses keep me company."

"So what do you do for sex?"

She spun round, stunned by the suddenness and

immediacy of the question.

"I mean, real sex," said Mandi. "Do you like to sleep with black men?"

Sta could not form a response. "I…" she stammered, shaking her head not in denial but for loss of words.

******

She remembered the time in London, visiting her sister. Anna was the brainy one. Educated, unlike Sta, in the UK at Millfield and then Trinity College, Oxford, Anna had stepped out of the colonial life and attitudes. Her friends were an eclectic mix of every race. Her partner Rambi was Indian. One evening, she had thrown a dinner party – Sta half suspected it was a matchmaking exercise, but she went along with it. She was a little tipsy by the time they sat down to dinner and she found herself next to Kennedy, a black Zambian.

"I hear Mugabe's had some sort of military complex built for the Chinese outside Harare," Kennedy was saying. "Do you think he's trying to sell the country to the Chinese, like they are doing in my country?"

Kennedy wore a blindingly colourful orange and green shirt outside his trousers. He was a big, swarthy, good-looking man with a deep-throated laugh like a chuckling hippo. It was so infectious that everyone at the table laughed with him.

Sta muttered something about her horses. She did not really take an interest in politics or the economy – she just loved Zim, whatever had happened, and immersed herself in her stable.

She realised, through the mist of the wine, that she was having an intelligent conversation with a black person, or, rather, he was making intelligent conversation with her.

This was not something that used to happen in her Zim.

"And what do you do?" she asked, in an effort to divert the wordflow.

It turned out that Kennedy was a banker but he could tell, she was sure, when he described his job, that she was not really interested in the intricacies of Standard Chartered and so they talked of other things – the wonder of the wildlife in the Kafue National Park in western Zambia, the problem of poaching, and some English friends who had started up a company called Tribal Textiles in Lusaka.

His voice was at once deep, soft and full. Sta was entranced and when he offered to share a taxi at the end of the evening, she was softly compliant. He put his arm around her shoulders as they got into the black cab and she snuggled silently into his warmth.

"So we're at my flat. Do you want the taxi to take you on to your hotel, or would you like to come in."

"I'll come in," she'd said, feeling reckless and powerless.

Kennedy was very gentle.

"Drink? Coffee?" He put some African music on.

She sat on one end of the sofa, her right leg crossed underneath her.

"Lovely coffee," she said .

"*You* are very lovely," said Kennedy, brushing the side of her face with his fingertips.

She leant into him and they kissed languidly. "You are a great big cuddly bear," said Sta. "And the first black man I've been with."

"First times are good," he said.

She started to unbutton his wild-coloured shirt and kissed his neck and his chest hungrily. But then she pulled back. Something was stopping her.

She looked at him, her eyes wide, searching his, feeling helpless and unknowing, unsure and unable to go on.

"It's OK," he said.

He kissed her hair and lifted her gently onto the bed, and when she woke the next morning, she had found a note. It said simply, 'Thank you, K'.

******

"So you are a racist," Mandi said, but it was not an accusation.

"No, I am *not* a racist," said Sta, forcefully.

To her surprise, Mandi opened her palms wide in a gesture of acceptance.

"Hey, I don't like to sleep with white men."

Sta flushed. An untidy jumble of papers sat on the kitchen table and, after setting down two cups of tea, she started to rifle through them, her confused thoughts and emotions a mirror image of their chaos.

Eventually she pulled out a sheet.

"You have a pen?" asked Mandi.

"Here."

She leant across. Sta's eyes were drawn to the shape of her breasts inside her patterned top, firm, smooth and black, and caught her breath. A mild amusement hung on Mandi's lips as she looked back at her, acknowledging silently the direction of Sta's gaze.

"The money will be in your bank tomorrow," she said, then stood up decisively and was gone.

Sta ruminated. Why had she felt uneasy with Kennedy, as if she was about to betray some unwritten law? Her parents had sent her to a boarding school in Bulawayo. She and Sophie had had that kind of mutual crush of course that she had never told anyone about. But didn't everyone at boarding school? It was just a teenage thing - wasn't it? And otherwise she had spent most of her young life at the Mvurwi Country Club. The tennis courts, golf course, cricket pitch and, most importantly, polo field had been haven for the teenage Sta. She had played polo for the under-20's men's team, and outrode most of them.

Sometimes, in some far corner of her mind, she had wondered how it was that all her friends were white Europeans, and all the farm workers, house boys, cooks, grooms and gardeners were black. But most of the time she had accepted this - it was the way. She was too busy enjoying her life and the attentions of the young men around her to question the situation, though she knew that changes were happening.

All that life had gone now, of course, the farm untended, the country club derelict and the sports fields overgrown. But Sta considered Zim her country and, post-Isaac, had used what little family money was left to buy the Chikuda stables. She had thrown herself into her horses - breeding, keeping them at livery, giving riding instruction - in a kind of quiet, civilized raging against the loss of innocence and questioning of what now should be.

So was she a racist? Ask Kennedy.

Or was it Mandi who was the racist, she thought to herself?

******

Sta went out to the yard in the early morning light and saddled up Sovereign. She was her joy and freedom and a dawn ride to the top of the escarpment was her favourite part of the day.

She was already up on the dark grey mare when she saw the lights of a vehicle coming through the gate. She sensed it was Mandi before she saw the colour of the Toyota.

She rode alongside and called out, "Want to ride up to the ridge?"

Mandi beamed. "I'll be right there."

Two of the grooms quickly helped Mandi tack up her new purchase and she was out in the yard within ten minutes. In beige jodhpurs, suede riding boots and blue fleece over a white blouse, she looked stunning, more like a model, even at this time in the morning, Sta thought – a contrast to herself in worn jeans and old hacking boots.

Beyond the gate, a few flame-red msasa trees lined the dirt track like a row of ill-disciplined sentries. Once clear of these the whole vista of the land opened up in front of them in faded shades of khaki , brown and dusty green. The grey of the escarpment stood as the horizon in this part of the country, testament to the farmlands beyond and savannah between. In the distance, they could see the round thatched huts of the village. Their route was flat for two or three miles, before a gradual incline and then the steep ascent to the top.

They rode in silence for a while, only the sound of stirrup leathers straining, the brushing of the horses' legs through the long, almost yellow, grass and the occasional cry of a child from the village disturbing the stillness of the African morning. The fresh smell of dawn, and vegetation that had slept, rose up to greet them and the tang of wood smoke hung in the air – the smell of home. Trotting sometimes, francolin scuttled out of the bush and insects flew up in clouds from the undergrowth.

As the ground inclined, they moved into a slow canter. When Sta looked across, Mandi had a broad grin on her face. "How's he going?" she asked.

"He's a dream. I'm going to call him Leo, just plain Leo

– forget Mr DiCaprio."

They reached a natural plateau below the final climb to the summit of the escarpment. A small lake had formed here and Sta let her horse drink.

She felt like a teenager again. "I'll race you to the top," she called out and nudged Sovereign in the belly, choosing a route up the steep incline. The mare quickened and began to devour the hill, picking her way over the scrub and the rocks. Sta could see Mandi to her left, Leo's chestnut mane flowing as he powered up a different track, then out of sight behind a rocky outcrop. She had to slow to a walk to negotiate a hidden gully and then, as she set off again, Mandi came cantering past laughing.

They high-fived and dismounted, tying the horses to a solitary acacia on the summit.

"You win," said Sta, pulling a water bottle from her saddle bag.

She lay back on the ground, amidst the swirls of flame lily and mountain grasses, taking a swig, then reached her arm across.

"Want some?"

Mandi drank and for some moments they lay in an effortless silence, filled only by the incessant hum of crickets and the occasional cry of a bird. The sun was already warming the earth as they surveyed the world below them. To the right lay fertile lands and, to the left, beyond the bush, the outskirts of Harare. A curl of smoke rose from the village.

What was it about this woman? Sta asked herself. Why was she so intoxicating?

A snake slithered across a nearby rock. For a second, she thought it was a puff adder, a vestige of fear from life on the farm kicking in before she realised it was just a harmless file snake.

A martial eagle wheeled and soared overhead, way up. Mandi watched it intently.

"I wonder what he thinks, when he sees us below. Does he think, 'Oh there's a white woman and a black woman', like he sees a chestnut horse and a grey horse?" said Sta.

"I don't think so," said Mandi. "I think he thinks 'Oh there's a *beautiful* white woman and a black woman.' "

"I can see a beautiful black woman."

Mandi leant across on her elbow and touched Sta's lips with her index finger.

Her pulse quickened. A fleeting memory of Sophie crossed her mind. She wanted to draw Mandi down into her, to bury herself in her. She looked up into her brown smiling eyes.

"I was thinking," she said playfully, "about what you said yesterday. You said I must be a racist. But you know, I think it is you who must be a racist. It was you who said you would not sleep with a white man."

A chuckle emanated from deep within Mandi.

Her right hand traced the curves of Sta's chest, lingering over the nipple of her left breast and moving up to her cheek.

"Man," she said. "White *man*. That was the important word."

12 EXTINCTION REBELLION

Bicycle tricycle
Up go the children
Up the path of the rainbow
Luminous blue

Look, sing the children
Apricot indigo
Look at the rainbow
The colours that glow

Know, cry the children
Gazing vermilion
Holding a mirror high
To their elders below

Days in the Life

See in the mirror, they say
Wounded the morning
Wounded by greedy men
Littermen thieves

Thieves of the songbirds
Thieves of the forests
Thieves of our future
Gone with the past

Gone to the cauldron, they say
Cinders and ashes
Gone to the cauldron
Where nothing will last

What were you thinking
They shout down from the rainbow
Shadowed the earth you've left
Shadowed our life at best.

ABOUT THE AUTHOR

After graduating from St Andrews with a degree in Modern History and Moral Philosophy, Tony Lindsell joined the Hertfordshire Gazette. He went on to write for, and ultimately edit, an alternative newspaper in London before becoming managing editor of Samsom Publications, a business newsletter publisher in the days before the internet.

He later moved out of journalism and, following an eclectic career, formed a company, Atlantic Equine Ltd, that specialises in equine hoofcare. He still runs that company but continues to write the occasional feature article. He has written for The Lady, Trainer, Horse and Hound and Warwickshire Life.

Fiction is a different art and Tony Lindsell has only been trying his hand at it for the last five years. Days in the Life is his first book of short stories and poems. He has also written a novel, Balmanie (see overleaf).

Days in the Life

BALMANIE (A preview)

An unseen and unnamed power strikes at the heart of Great Britain and spreads quickly throughout the country. The electricity supply goes down. All forms of communication - mobile, internet, satellite, TV, radio, landline - fail. Police, army, government and hospitals are rendered helpless. Mains water is poisoned and many people die. Chaos and anarchy quickly take hold.

Sam and his girlfriend Shani flee north from London to the house of his parents - Henry, recently retired, and Josephine, who suffers from depression. That house, in turn, is overrun by others escaping the capital. The family become refugees in their own country. Piling into a Toyota Landcruiser, they head for Balmanie, on the island of Mull, where Henry's sister, Anne-Marie, lives.

A Syrian refugee, Rabiyah, her baby and two young students, Stef and Lou, join them. Armed only with a shotgun and a farmer's rifle, they fight their way towards Scotland. Dark drones and helicopters appear in the sky above them, as if ghosting their journey.

On Mull, Anne-Marie allows the peace-loving, vegetarian followers of Baba Ji to share the house. The devotees are led by the mysterious and alluring Mira. Together, Anne-Marie hopes that they can protect Balmanie and its precious well from marauders, if not from the drones and helicopters that loom here too.

The travelling group encounter hardships, difficulties and moral dilemmas at every stage of the way. In the battle to survive, the abhorrent becomes normal.

The two lines of the story converge on the Balmanie beach. Though the family and the devotees begin to work together, they are left in a kind of limbo. The drones taunt them. Balmanie is not the safe haven they hoped it would be. Where will the next meal come from? How long will it be before they are attacked? Where can they run to? Can Baba Ji save them? How will the guns be used?

Printed in Poland
by Amazon Fulfillment
Poland Sp. z o.o., Wrocław

52072577R00063